CHARMING THE CURSE'S CONSORT

Aralian Series Novella - Book 1.5

Chelle Cypress

Chelle Cypress

Cover by Amber Thoma

Edited by:
Brittany Mack (Developmental Editing) & Beth Lawton (Copy Edit/Proofread)

ISBN: 979-8-9891185-3-3

DEDICATION

In loving memory of my dear friend Christy. My deepest regret is rescheduling our last walk. I wish I could go back in time so I could have that final hike, to say goodbye. Thank you for being my friend and the kindest soul I've ever met.

CONTENT WARNING

Alcohol Consumption, Blood, Brainwashing, Cult/High Control Religion, Death/Loss (Mention of loss of partner & parents), Depression, Disappearance of Loved One, Forced Servitude (Mentioned through flash backs), Greif/Loss, Grooming (Implied through flash backs), Homelessness (Mention of), Infertility (Mention of), Physical Abuse (Mentioned in flash backs), Sexual Coercion/Ambiguous Consent (Implied in flash backs), Sexually Explicit Scenes, Terminal Illness, Violence (Mentioned in flash backs), Whipping (Mentioned in flash backs)

CHAPTER 1

THE KESERE FESTIVAL

BRIELLE

LOVE HAD FINALLY PREVAILED.

My nose wrinkled at the ridiculous thought. When had I become so soft? The old me wouldn't have given a flying fig if Silas and Arianna had acknowledged their connection. Yet here I stood, among the shadows, a few paces away from the alley where they hid, eavesdropping on their interaction. Goosebumps crawled over my skin as my bare shoulder pressed against the frigid stone building. Seconds skittered past, then moans echoed through the night, confirming that they'd indeed accepted their bond. A smirk tugged on my lips at their amorous activities, but they'd likely prefer their privacy.

I spun and headed in the opposite direction, down the cobble path that led to the Kesere festival. Muffled music drifted through the atmosphere from the celebration ahead. The crisp late-autumn air filled my lungs, yet the tension in my body didn't ease now that the pair wouldn't be pestering me. Instead, a pang tugged at my heart. I tried to ignore the ache, but it had only grown over the past few months, as Arianna and Silas's love story unfolded. Their mating had dredged up memories that were best left buried of my own long-lost beloved, Wren. Summoned by thoughts of her, a hard knot formed in my throat. I swallowed it, unwilling to relent to the bubbling recollections threatening to burst through the dam I'd built in order to survive.

Desperate for distraction, I hastened my pace. A minute later, a cacophony of chatter melded with the fiddler's tune as I entered the festivities. Heat radiated from the steel fire pits encircling the boisterous celebrations sprawling across the main street. I dodged a gaggle of mothers playing with their laughing children who congregated near the crackling blaze. Then I made my way to the square to search for my current bedfellow. To my displeasure, Everette danced with the voluptuous Violetta Vasquez. From his tight grasp upon her rear, he'd found another. A twinge of agitation flared but extinguished. Hours prior, he'd made his intentions to marry soon clear—a desire I didn't share. Apparently, Violetta had caught his attention. They'd likely be wed by spring, just as many of the newly formed couples from Kesere, Presspin's unofficial matchmaking ceremony.

Undeterred, I beelined for the refreshment table near the water fountain. If I couldn't have distraction in a warm body, then I'd find solace in a drink. I pushed through the onlookers, then skirted around the tables brimming with revelers partaking of the feast. My empty stomach growled over the thick tang of beef and ale wafting through the air. I licked my lips, but the sensation of eyes burning on my back caused me to slow my pace.

"Did you see Brielle chasing after Lord and Lady Belmont? We all knew he wouldn't keep her as his mistress after bringing his pretty bride home," a viper whispered loud enough for me to hear.

"And her new beau abandoned her, too," another harpy tittered.

Annoyance blossomed. I'd endured a ridiculous amount of gossip since coming to Presspin. Most of the rumors were twisted to entertain the hordes. Yet these ladies obviously desired a show. Willing myself to relax, my fists unclenched at my side and my hands smoothed over the black lace fabric clinging to my hips. Then I tossed my auburn locks. Certain that the sensual motions drew attention, I peeked over my bare shoulder to where they sat. To my fortune, their husbands lounged beside them, panting over my sultry form. I winked at the group. The women squawked at their partners like the hens they were. Yet their anger toward their spouses held little satisfaction.

I suppressed my increasing vexation with the evening and approached the refreshments. Roasted meats, vegetables, and a plethora of decadent desserts were picked clean through. Candlelight sparkled against the crystal brimming with spiced wine. My fingers itched for relief. I clutched the glass's stem and breathed in the heady cinnamon aroma.

"Drowning your sorrows now that no one wants you? Oh, how the mighty have fallen."

My spine stiffened at Rosalind Collins's screech. As Presspin's primary gossipmonger, she spread tales like a farmer spread manure. To my misfortune, she'd set her frustration upon me after I'd reported her husband's lecherous advances to Lord Belmont. The potbellied Mr. Collins, the former bank manager, believed my lack of coin meant I would cavort with him in lieu of collateral for my herbalist shop. Though the incident left a sour first impression of the village, it had led me to forming a friendship with the brooding Silas.

I took a sip of the spiced beverage to wash away the distasteful memory. These games were tiresome, and I opted to ignore her. Hopefully, she'd leave me to enjoy my libation in peace.

Tap. Tap. Tap. Her tiny, booted feet clipped on the stone. She assumed I owed her my attention.

The cinnamon flavor bittered on my tongue. I cared little about her ire for me, but the burgeoning memories of Wren, my lack of a paramour, the gabbing biddies, and being unable to drown my feelings in drink had diminished my resolve. Unbeknownst to her, Rosalind Collins would be the antidote for my displeasure.

I spun and faced the pest. The thirty-five-year-old seemed matronly, with her downturned pout, tightly woven chignon, and washed-out complexion. She squirmed under my perusal of her form, then straightened. Her discomfort egged me on. I closed the distance between us with a catlike grace, certain to add an extra sway to my hips. I halted before her, close enough to count the constellation of freckles dotting her button nose. She inhaled sharply. Was her frustration pent-up sexual tension?

Her breath quickened. Desperation rolled off her. But I had a code of ethics—no affairs. Though I'd tiptoed that boundary when I'd kissed Silas in the library, which had been a sly ploy to drive Arianna into a jealous rage. However, the pair had been foolish to the end, denying their love until now. Perhaps Rosalind, too, needed a bit of a push.

My fingers trailed along a stray lock that had escaped her tight knot. "Oh, Rosalind. I'm not the only one those hens have been clucking over. Everyone's been talking about how your best friend, Corina Cummings, has been entangling with your husband."

Silence stretched as the once chattering chits at the nearby tables watched on. Rosalind smacked my hand away. Her once lustful gaze hardened to one of hatred. Her nostrils flared, and her features pinched, creating fine creases throughout her pale skin. She jutted her chin skyward and stomped away, only to career straight into a gentleman sipping ale. His beer splashed over the edge, splattering the dark substance into her blonde hair. She shuddered but continued her warpath into the square. A shrieking note screeched as the fiddling ceased. Shouts filled the air. All eyes shifted from me and onto the arguing couple.

I turned away, uncaring as Rosalind confronted her husband and best friend. Instead, I gulped the drink, then placed my empty glass on the table. Free from the blathering hordes, I plucked a citrus biscuit and nibbled on it, ignoring the unfolding chaos.

A minute later, the music recommenced, and my beloved's song played. The small bit of dessert lodged in my throat. I swallowed hard. Panic coiled within me. My pulse panged to the beat of the song I'd danced to mere minutes before glimpsing Wren for the first time. Goose bumps rose on my skin, and I swore Wren's voice called my name through the bitter breeze. Unsettled, I laid my half-eaten delicacy on the table. I needed to rid my mind of memories of her, and the best way to do so was to find a new bedfellow. Desperately, I scanned the festival, but to my horror, everyone had paired off, leaving me alone.

Each mournful note caused my well-buried emotions to eke closer to the surface, like a jack-in-the-box ready to burst free by the end of the macabre tune. A shudder crawled along my spine. I needed to regroup. Appearing unbothered, I swayed through the revelers, akin to my nights dancing for dignitaries at the temple. The crowd parted, and I slipped into the shadows. In the cloak of night, the weight of my performance dissipated.

The darkness enveloped me, causing a shiver to snake along my spine. Yet this icy chill resided internally, only to be dulled by the blaze of carnal entanglements.

Fatigued, I trudged toward a shadowed building and rested against the frigid brick. Overwhelmed, I closed my eyes, but Wren lived behind my eyelids. My heart pounded. Wren's face popped into my mind. Her violet irises, her smooth, sepia skin, her lush black locks. Pain burned in my throat, and the hollow ache her absence caused clawed at me, attempting to take hold.

"I'd never guess you to be a wallflower, Ms. Brielle." A masculine voice pierced through my thoughts.

Jarred from the past and thrust into the empty present, I couldn't muster my siren performance. Temporarily untethered from my persona, a fraction of my true self slithered through the cracks of my facade. "I'm just taking a break."

"Me too." A weary vulnerability entered the man's voice.

Surprised by the genuineness, I pivoted toward him, but shadows obscured his face.

Unwilling to share my inner world, I buried my feelings and forced a flirtatious lilt. "I'm exhausted from being berated by so many eager partners."

"Is that so?" Disbelief coated his tone.

The swipe of a match catching along the stone drew my attention. A small flame flickered to life in his grip. He lit a cigarette tucked between his full lips, and my focus lingered on his long fingers as he plucked it from his mouth. He reached overhead, alighting the sconce between us.

My brain bottled my thoughts of Wren and focused on the dashing gentleman before me. I needed a bedfellow, and Mateo Reed had stumbled upon me, guided by fate herself. I'd seen him milling about the town. Due to the man being twenty-two—six years my junior—I hadn't paid him any mind. Truly taking him in now, that had been a dreadful mistake. The faint light from the torch overhead caressed his sharp jaw and washed over his defined cheekbones. I'd once thought his hair to be a bland brunette, but against the red brick wall, pops of chestnut wove through his wavy tresses. A morose mood replaced his usually good-natured aura. This uncharacteristic broody demeanor possessing him this evening made him appear older.

On the prowl, I sauntered to him. "And what about you? Why are you hiding? Isn't there a horde of young ladies who'd be elated if you filled their dance cards?" My finger trailed along his firm chest, tracing over the gray button of his wool coat.

Slowly, he removed the cigarette from his delectable mouth, dropped it to the ground, and twisted his heavy boot over the butt. "Honestly, Kesere isn't the same. Not since Ingrid passed."

As if I'd been doused with cold water, my hand fell limp to my side. How could I have forgotten? His childhood sweetheart and betrothed had died nearly a year ago from complications from influenza.

"My condolences. Ingrid was a lovely girl," I said, knowing I'd done my best to help the frail woman.

Wordlessly, he tilted his gaze skyward, studying the stars overhead, as if he could see her through the veil between this plane and the Great Beyond. I should leave, but it seemed that we both needed solace this evening. Perhaps, a night together would act as a balm for our shared grief.

I stepped closer until my body lingered near inches from his. My thumb grazed over his charcoal lapel. Then my palm settled upon his chest, and his heart thumped wildly. His focus shifted from the sky and onto me.

"Why don't we head to my apartment for a nightcap?"

He placed his hand on mine, and a thrill rushed through me. "Why do you want to leave?"

A wrinkle formed between my brows. Had these bothersome emotions leaked out? My expression pinched.

"What's bothering you?" He studied me.

"I'm fine." I withdrew. A burning need to run fueled me.

"Then why are you hiding here instead of partaking in the festivities?"

A plucky country tune twanged, filling the crisp air. My brain reeled. If I fled, it would confirm his suspicions. I had no inclination to reenter the celebration, but I wouldn't allow him or anyone to see an ounce of vulnerability. I plastered on my sultry persona and purred. "Shall we dance, then?"

An awkward beat of silence passed. Fortunately, he reached for me, lacing his fingers with mine. Heat radiated into my icy palms. Despite having been touched in far more salacious ways, his calluses caused a wave of warmth to wash over me. My heart pounded as he led me out of the darkness and into the light.

We weaved past the fires and the onlooking horde. All the while, I ignored the bubbling murmurs of the golden boy and the wicked seductress. Unruffled by the floating rumors, he peered over his shoulder, checking to make sure I was unbothered by their gossip.

Moments later, we settled onto the square. The other dancers moved in unison, bouncing through the jig. His large hand skidded over the fitted lace of my dress and rested on the curve of my hip. Heat pooled in my core at the thought of his digits slipping farther south. Instinctively, my palm skimmed over the thick wool coat clinging to his frame and found its place on the crook of his back. His free hand clasped mine, uniting us in this quick-stepped set. Without missing a beat, he whirled me into the sea of dancers, falling smoothly in line.

He moved with a fluid ease, as if music pulsed in his blood. Most men had a refined stiffness, but Mateo glided with unhurried grace. I loved to dance, and it had been an age since I'd had such a skilled partner.

Minutes seemed like seconds as colors swirled, blurring the world. My pulse rose with each pluck the fiddler made. The melody wrapped around us, creating a cocoon of beating rhythms. A bubbling laugh escaped me. Why did I feel so relaxed?

He chuckled. The velvety-smooth timbre sent a flutter to pulse in my belly. "Dancing can be just as enjoyable as a nightcap." His hazel eyes twinkled with a hint of mischief.

I arched an eyebrow, intrigued that he had brought up my earlier offer. He hadn't rejected my initial advance. Perhaps, due to his age and inexperience, he needed a more direct approach. Attempting to ensnare him again, I pressed into him. My cheek grazed his stubbled jaw. "You know what they say. A couple whose bodies move in sync on the dance floor will also find themselves in raptures when writhing in bed."

"Is that so? And what about after their entanglement? What then?" He cocked his head to the side, causing his wavy locks to shift.

"After..." Didn't the whole town know of my rules? My paramours weren't allowed to linger for postcoital cuddles.

Flummoxed, my brain faltered. The music's pace quickened, signaling a partner change. Thrown off-kilter by my milling thoughts, I haphazardly whirled toward an awaiting woman. My heel caught in a crack in the cobblestone and snapped clean off. I teetered precariously. Luckily, I found my footing before toppling over. Guffawing echoed over the music. Apparently, the townsfolk watching from the sidelines were unimpressed. Ignoring the simpletons, I bent to retrieve my fractured footwear but stopped as my gaze locked with Mateo's. To my astonishment, he knelt before me with the broken slipper in his outstretched palm.

"Well, this will not do." His thumb traced along my ankle.

He cradled my foot and replaced my shoe.

"I'm uninjured. I—"

He lifted me in one fell swoop.

"I can walk."

"Oh, I'm sure you can hobble the three blocks to your herbalist shop. We all know you don't need help from anyone. But just this once, can you allow me to assist you?" Without awaiting my answer, he strode through the revelers, who gawked as we made our abrupt exit.

Maybe this was Mateo's plan—to act as the gallant knight, taking the fair maiden to safety, while, in reality, he needed an excuse for depositing me in my bed. Certain this walk would result in us entangling, I leaned my head against his chest and inhaled his scent, a mix of mint and sage. Soon, his aroma would live on my sheets, as we spent the night lost in each other.

Minutes later, the flickering lamplight washed over my familiar stone home. My pulse rose, excited at the prospect of discovering pleasure with a new partner. He approached the outer stairs with fluid ease and scaled the steps at a careful pace. Yearning built with each passing second. However, when we reached the landing, he lowered me to my feet.

"It's best I leave you here. Thank you for your company this evening." Despite the statement, he didn't move from the spot.

To my understanding, Ingrid had been his sole lover. Was he uncertain how to initiate a more casual interlude? My fist wrapped around the knob. "The night doesn't have to end. Come inside, and I'll help you forget about the ghosts haunting you."

To my surprise, his right foot landed on the step behind him, creating space between us. "That's tempting, but I made a promise to Ingrid before she died." His eyes darted toward the moon, and a bit of a blush colored his pale complexion. He inhaled sharply, whatever he had to say seemed to pain him. "I promised her I'd remain chaste until I fell in love again."

I opened my mouth to speak, but clamped it shut. I could provide him with carnal pleasure, but nothing more. I nodded in understanding, but for some reason, the rejection hurt akin to a knife in my gut. My fingers unlocked the door. The click punctuated the awkward silence. My foot crossed the threshold.

"Wait." He held up his hands, halting me. "It's a vow I intend to keep, but I would like to become better acquainted with you." He rubbed the nape of his neck, reminding me of his youth.

He scrubbed a hand through his hair, seeming a bit fidgety. Was he working through some moral loophole which would allow him satisfaction while keeping his promise? He continued to surprise me when he blurted out. "I want to court you."

My nose crinkled at the old-fashioned proposal. Sensing my thoughts, he gave a halfhearted shrug. A bone-weary sigh escaped me. However, given the events of tonight, the way the entire town paired off for the season, my winter would be tedious. I should say no, but he'd said nothing about me loving him in return. Instead of denying him, I crooned, "Perhaps."

CHAPTER 2

MATEO

SHADOWS CLUNG TO THE memory marker tucked into the depths of the woods. My eyes grew misty, and my nostrils stung. In the past, I may have lied to myself that the whipping wind had caused these sniffles, but in truth, I missed Ingrid. Yet she wasn't lounging here beneath her favorite tree, with charcoal drenching her fingers, sketching the birds who'd settled on the branches overhead. Instead, a tombstone denoted her final resting place, where her ashes were scattered.

"Hello, sweetheart." I squatted and lowered the bouquet of daisies onto the snow-covered ground. My gloved hand dusted the accumulating flurries off the granite, then drifted over her name. A pang twisted in my gut. However, the ache now felt akin to an old wound that occasionally flared. When she'd first passed, I'd come here daily. Eventually, my visits dwindled into a weekly chat where I'd come to recount the town's tales, pretending to amuse her with anecdotes she would have loved. Despite occupying my time with renovating our farmhouse and collecting stories for her, I struggled to forge a new life. Until now.

I'd come to inform Ingrid of my formal pursual of Brielle, but a strange sensation of guilt tightened my chest. I'd expressed my interest in the herbalist during my past visits, often recounting my small interactions with Brielle, which likely went unnoticed by the siren but fueled my increasing interest. However, admitting to Ingrid that I'd indeed acted upon those feelings acknowledged my future without her, and that tasted of betrayal.

With my present deposited, I stood, then walked to the pine and leaned against it. The breeze blew, causing the petals on the chipper yellow flowers to shift against the gray granite. A knot formed in my throat. How was I supposed to have this conversation with the ground? Closing my eyes, I imagined Ingrid's face—the light cascading over her buttercream hair, her fair complexion, her arched nose, and her warm chocolate-brown irises. But I still couldn't muster the strength to voice the truth. Instead, I avoided my purpose for the visit and spoke about the Kesere festival nights ago.

Half an hour passed as I recounted leading Lady Belmont out in the first set, the festivities, and the way Lord Belmont strode across the dance floor to confront a stranger who'd flirted with his wife. Ingrid would have adored the chaos that ensued. Eventually, I delved into the incident involving Rosalind Collins, which led me straight to the topic of Brielle. My mouth dried, but I pressed on, knowing I had to divulge this information.

"The entire festival screeched to a halt as the Collinses bickered in the square. Brielle had caused quite a stir." My fingers scratched at the stubble on my chin. "But the ruckus stopped Vincent and Liam from pestering me about joining the boxing club. You know I'm not much of a fighter, but the pair had me on the ropes, pun fully intended. Once the music restarted, they left me in search of dessert, and I shuffled to the shadows for a cigarette."

I could almost hear her chastising me over the nasty habit.

"Yes, I'm aware that you don't approve. Please understand, I was missing you during that long, lonely night." I shrugged, then continued. "Right before I lit my cigarette, Brielle strode toward me and settled against the wall a mere few feet away. I should have made my presence known, but I froze. She stood there, unmoving, in the dark. Minutes passed, and I fumbled with what to say. Unable to bear the silence any longer, I said something idiotic about her being a wallflower."

Then what happened? Ingrid would have asked. For a moment, it felt like we were truly having a conversation.

I recounted the evening, from Brielle's morose mood in the shadows and spanning through events that led me to carrying her to her doorstep. I'd reached the moment of truth and paused. My shoulders tensed.

Go on. It's all right. You can tell me anything. Ingrid's voice echoed internally.

I gulped down the swelling knot. I loved Ingrid but had pined in silence over Brielle for months. Ingrid, of all people, saw the woman for who she truly was, and I hoped she wouldn't fault me for pursuing her.

I sucked in a breath and forced the words out. "I asked Brielle if I could court her. And she said *perhaps*."

A giggle flittered through my soul, as if Ingrid had heard my confession and found it amusing.

Ease coursed through my body. With the secret revealed, I proceeded. "I should be grateful for her *perhaps*, given my vow of chastity. Luckily, she didn't simply reject me." I'd dwelled on that small kernel of hope for the past few days. However, the aghast expression she'd worn when I said *court* had given me pause. "Since she seems skittish, I've been giving her space to process my request."

I waited for an acknowledgment from Ingrid. Instead, a gust blew, whipping powder over my face, forcing my awareness back onto the outside world. By habit, I searched the space for her, but my beloved was gone. Despite the external chill, a warmth filled my soul in answer. She'd wanted me to move on. Hadn't that been why she'd had me make that promise—that I'd remain chaste until I found love again?

A crow cawed overhead, drawing my attention. I tilted my head skyward, taking in the rolling black clouds blocking the once soft sunlight. A storm was brewing.

"I'd better go." I placed my gloved fingertips to my lips, pressing a soft kiss upon them. "Until next time, sweetheart." My fingers trailed over the stone, then I strode back toward the land of the living.

I trudged through the calf-deep snow, weaving around the dense evergreens for a quarter of an hour, until the divide between the woods and the outer world came into view.

I paused at the intersection. I could veer left toward home or right into the village. Brielle might need more time to consider my proposition, but time was fleeting. One moment, you could be wrapped in your lover's arms, and the next, have them ripped from you in a cruel twist of fate. Emboldened by my visit to Ingrid's grave, I headed for her shop. My mind whirled with how to explain my sudden appearance. Maybe I could feign a malady?

With a sense of urgency, I weaved through the townsfolk milling about the square, either venturing home or to the Owl's Nest for lunch. A nervous energy surged through my pulse, matching my clipped pace. Villagers glanced as I rushed past them, moving too quickly for the slick sidewalk. I didn't care.

Minutes later, the storefront came into view. My boot slid along the icy path leading to the entrance, but I stopped, taking in the sign on the door. *Closed until further notice.*

Worry replaced my eagerness. I read the note a dozen times, as if the four words held more meaning, yet they didn't. My shoulders slumped, uncertain what to do.

"Mateo! You all right?" a woman called from behind me.

"I'm fine." I spun back to the street and took in Layla's unusually grim expression.

A furrow creased between her brows. "Oh dear, I'm guessing you haven't heard the latest news, then."

I'd sequestered myself in my home since the festival and hadn't ventured into town until now. A pang of worry coursed through me. Had something happened to Brielle?

"It's Lord and Lady Belmont." Layla stepped closer, worry dampening her countenance. "The morning after the Kesere festival, word came from Krella that Arianna's mother was on her deathbed. Of course, my dear friends rushed home to say goodbye before the woman succumbed to her illness. But on their return to Presspin, they began showing symptoms of the same pneumonia that had taken the life of Arianna's mother. They are both extremely ill. Beatrix had to accompany the group here and fears the worst for her brother. Apparently, they both arrived here in a coma. Though Arianna is awake, Silas remains trapped in unconsciousness. It's dreadful. I'm going there this afternoon to take Naomi, Arianna's sister, winter clothing. Brielle's been staying at the manor and tending to the ailing pair. I can ask Brielle to send a tonic if you are in need."

I rubbed my nape, processing this information. Though I wanted to see Brielle, with the current emergency, she needed to focus on caring for the Belmonts. She possessed a skill I appreciated, having watched her usher Ingrid into the Great Beyond with gentle care. I'd wait until she was available again, then make my move.

"Thank you, but there's no need to bother Ms. Brielle." With a watery smile, I breezed by Layla and turned down the street to head back home.

CHAPTER 3

BRIELLE

I KICKED OFF MY boots, leaving them sprawled haphazardly inches from the entrance to my quarters. Exhausted, I stumbled forward and flopped onto the unmade bed, breathing in the cotton. My nose wrinkled at the musty sheets, and I rolled onto my back. My focus traced along the swirled pattern on the ceiling, hoping the repetitive motion would lull me into a deep slumber. Yet my mind still reeled from the events of this morning, making rest impossible.

Today, weeks since the Belmonts' return to Presspin after the incident in Daviel, Silas had risen like some fairy-tale prince breaking a sleeping curse. Despite Arianna's hope, I'd prepared myself for his passing, certain he wouldn't awaken. Shock had seized me when Mrs. Potter sprinted down the steps and skidded through the foyer to halt me from leaving, shouting that Lord Belmont had regained consciousness. I'd returned to his side and examined him. He'd lost muscle mass, and his movements were sluggish, but he'd been of sound mind. Once I'd declared him stable, Lady Belmont had shooed me out of his suite. I didn't blame her for wanting to revel in his revival. Yet a pang of jealousy clenched within my gut. Why hadn't a miracle occurred to save my beloved? I blinked back the sense of dread that, if I remained curled on the mattress with only my painful memories as company, they would swallow me whole.

Agitated, I sprang to my feet and stripped out of my work attire, uncaring as the pants and tunic crumpled onto the plush green rug. My feet padded along the lush carpet, weaving around the dirty clothing dotting the floor. The mess needed to be rectified, yet I had more pressing matters to attend to. After these exhaustingly long weeks caring for the Belmonts, I required a stiff drink and an even stiffer cock to occupy my newly freed time.

Determined to secure a new paramour, my hand wrapped around the brass knob of the wardrobe and tugged it open. Only three evening gowns remained. I huffed. I should have sent the dirty clothes to the laundress days ago, but I'd been too exhausted, having spent my days at the manor, then hav-ing barely enough energy to slip into a fitful sleep. My glance shifted to the window, where faint streams of sunlight broke through the clouds. It was too early for these dresses, but I had no desire to forgo my plans. Decisively, my fingers trailed over a velvet green garment thick enough to endure the snow while boasting a low neckline to entice a partner.

Hope blossomed, and I tugged the garment off the hanger and slipped it on. A couple must have broken off their tryst since Kesere. Harkened by the memory of the festival, Mateo popped into my mind. My lips pursed. An aching guilt clawed at me. I should have said no instead of *perhaps* when he'd requested to court me. That night, the memories of Wren had haunted me so deeply that I'd considered allowing him to fall in love with me while I remained unchanged. It was best to avoid Mateo Reed, despite his strong arms, handsome face, lithe form...no.

I shook my head, freeing myself from thoughts of the charming man, then turned toward the dressing table to prepare myself for the hunt. The vintage vanity sat opposite the wardrobe, tucked into a corner next to a window. Cream wallpaper with an ivy pattern covered the walls, the subdued colors making the dark wooden frame pop. As I reached the dressing table, my fingers trailed over my perfumes. I selected a mix of vanilla and amber, then rubbed the fragrance over my heat points, certain the alluring scent would capture someone's attention. Quickly, I unraveled my braid, pulled the silver comb from the drawer, and brushed my locks. Finally, I applied rouge to highlight my features. Satisfied, I yanked on my shoes, grabbed my cloak, and headed out of my apartment.

The bright sunlight cut through the thick storm clouds looming overhead, warming the bitter early winter afternoon. The yeasty scent of bread wafted from the nearby bakery, and my stomach grumbled. Yet I wouldn't be able to satisfy both my hungers here. Despite the delectable pastries displayed in the window, I pressed forward, weaving through the villagers, certain to add a bit of sway to my step. Men gawked at me while their wives tilted their chins to the sky with disdain. A smirk curled my lips. Certainly, my flamboyant costume would capture a new bedfellow.

Minutes later, hoots echoed from the Owl's Nest straight ahead. The stone and basalt building stood two stories high, housing the inn above and the tavern below. Lamp light streamed through the sparkling windows, highlighting the dwellers imbibing within. The typically subdued space became boisterous each winter, since the farmers had little to do except eat, drink, and make merry during the snowy months.

I approached, then pushed into the building. The usually occupied inn's welcome desk sat empty, given the lack of visitors during these icy months. The sweet aroma of honey buns mixed with the bitter tang of fresh ale harkened me forward into the tavern. The sleek mahogany bar sat to my right, with bottles of liquor lining the walls, while round tables filled with villagers dotted the rest of the space. A deafening cheer echoed from a cluster to my left, where a crowd of elderly farmers encircled a beaming Mr. Johnson, who'd won a round of dominos. I weaved around another group of middle-aged men playing billiards and headed toward the back corner that housed an alcove where younger patrons congregated.

I licked my lips and painted on my most alluring smile. My heart raced in anticipation. Who would I lure into my bed today? The raucous laughter dampened as I entered the secluded spot that offered a more intimate space for young folk to connect.

My excitement faltered. Couples cuddled at every table, as if I'd stepped into some lovers' den. I bit the inside of my cheek, stifling my fury. Gods, there wasn't an unpaired soul here. But the lunch hour had just begun. Perhaps a solo patron would arrive. Until then, I'd occupy my time with a whiskey. I smoothed my expression, pressed my shoulders back, and headed for the bar. Not a single glance shifted to me, but at least there was no need to perform. I settled on the high stool, propped an elbow on the slick mahogany countertop, and leaned my chin into my cupped hand. Fiona, the tavern maid, approached.

"We haven't seen you out and about since Kesere." She grabbed a glass, spun toward the bottles covering the back wall, and selected an expensive bottle of booze with a gold-encrusted label.

I arched an eyebrow as she filled a snifter with two fingers of the amber liquid.

"On the house. How's Lord Belmont?" She slid the spirit to me.

"Awake and well." My fingers pressed against the cut crystal, trailing over the intricate swirling pattern. I lifted the whiskey, breathed in the sharp scent, and took a sip. Warmth pooled in my belly, loosening my tension.

"Aye, that's excellent news." Fiona poured herself a serving and raised it to the patrons. "To Lord Belmont."

"To Lord Belmont," the crowd cheered in unison.

"To Lord Belmont," I whispered, then took a long swig.

Fiona sauntered away to assist another purchasing lunch for their sweetheart. Without any company, I couldn't suppress the niggling thought. How had Silas survived the blast? I swirled my drink, studying it as if it held the answers to my quandary.

Moments later, a hand rested on my shoulder, pulling me from my ruminations. A shiver snaked along my spine, then coursed akin to lightning through my skin, setting my body ablaze. Apparently, my assumption had been correct. Someone had sought me out. I downed the remaining liquor, certain whoever had created this reaction in me would soon be in my bed.

I spun, taking in Mateo's handsome face.

"May I join you?"

I should decline him, but his warm hazel eyes drank me in like I was some mystical being, and that dang crooked smile crested over his lips, disarming me.

"Glad to see you've returned to your jovial self and are no longer brooding in the shadows." I shouldn't flirt with him, but I couldn't help myself.

His grin widened, lightening his face, and his hazel eyes crinkled with mirth. "I thought you preferred your men dark and moody."

I snorted, amused that he could keep up with my wit. "Not particularly. Though a brooding bedfellow can be entertaining at times."

As soon as the word *bedfellow* tumbled from me, his light-hearted features tightened. What was I doing? This man couldn't offer me primal companionship, and I couldn't offer him my heart. I needed to focus on my task of securing someone else. However, given the room full of canoodling couples, this afternoon would likely be a dull one. Sensing his stare, my attention shifted back to Mateo. What was the harm of allowing him to sit beside me?

"Fine." I waved to the seat next to mine.

His expression brightened, like sunshine on a cold winter's day. He settled on the stool and gestured to Fiona for a drink. "I tried to stop by the shop after the Kesere festival, but you were at the manor. I assume Lord and Lady Belmont are well again?"

An awkward silence washed over us. He'd sought me out and likely still hoped to court me. I spun toward him, needing to clarify that he shouldn't hope for anything more than a casual acquaintanceship. He beamed, looking like a sweet puppy ready to play. My resolve melted at the earnest expression. My fingernails drummed against the mahogany top as my mind tried to concoct a plan to let him down easily.

My tone took on a serious note. "He's alive. But Mateo, I've been thinking about your proposition. I don't—"

"I was too forward, asking to court you. Instead, let me keep you company this winter?" He frowned, and his shoulders slumped.

Thankfully, Fiona returned and placed an ale before Mateo. She refilled my snifter, then scurried away. A solemn aura settled around us. My lips flattened. Swiftly, I picked up the liquor and kicked it back. The contents burned down my throat, further loosening my inhibitions.

Mateo's fingers traced along the rim of his glass. "Or I can leave if you'd prefer."

I scrubbed a hand over my face, having no desire to sit here alone. Hadn't that been why I'd come to seek distraction? Perhaps chatting with him wouldn't be a bad way to pass the time. "You can stay for now, but if someone approaches me..." My fingers pressed into my temples, and my brain buzzed from the two spirits I'd had on an empty stomach. "But who will seek me out when a handsome man is seated beside me?"

Delight replaced his sulking expression. "So you think I'm handsome?"

I rolled my eyes. My stomach grumbled, protesting on my behalf. His glance shot to my gut. A sly smile tugged on the corner. "Come on, now. Let me buy you lunch and a whole tray of honey buns."

Unbeknownst to him, he'd caught me with the proposition of sweets. My mouth watered. Though I couldn't fill my bed, at least I could fill my belly. "Fine, but I'm not sharing my treats."

CHAPTER 4

BRIELLE

MY STOMACH GRUMBLED IN protest at the *Closed* wooden sign on the door of the Owl's Nest. My fingers pinched the bridge of my nose, as pangs pulsed through my empty belly. Today had been terrible. I'd forgone eating breakfast, rushing at the crack of dawn to set little Timothy Tilbert's broken leg instead of heading to the grocer. Then I'd completed the rounds, tending to three families who suffered from a sudden head cold sweeping through the town. I worked my jaw. Had it not been enough that everyone remained coupled, forcing me into this sexual drought? Now the solace of a warm meal and whiskey had been taken from me too?

Boots sloshed behind me. "That's a shame."

I spun toward Mateo, and sunlight glimmered, lighting his chestnut locks. His gray coat clung to him, and my fingers itched to unbutton it and see what laid beneath. My mouth watered. Gods, I was ravenous. I could devour him and a tray of honey buns too. But despite this gnawing need, I wouldn't tarnish his vow to Ingrid with a casual interlude. Somehow, I'd grown fond of the man as we'd eaten lunch together daily for nearly a fortnight. The realization caused a nervous energy to bubble within me. I shuddered, then shook my head, dislodging the swirling thoughts.

He studied me, and his smile fell. "You look pale. Are you unwell?"

My nose wrinkled in consternation, then I opened my mouth to volley a retort, but my belly growled in my stead.

"Have you eaten today?" Mateo scrubbed his chin as his gaze remained fixed on me.

"I haven't, but there's a jar of pickles and whiskey waiting for me at home." My lips pursed at the thought of an unsatisfactory meal. Yet being left wanting had been a sudden theme in my life.

"First, that isn't enough nourishment. Second, pickles and whiskey sound like a terrible combination." His good-natured features tightened, and a hint of something far more determined entered his hazel eyes.

For a heartbeat, desire surged forward. My brain skittered toward a curiosity that had crossed my mind more than once—did his gentle demeanor to the outside world match his nature in bed? Yet, from the tightness in his jaw, perhaps a dominant streak roiled within? Thoughts of him overtaking me flooded my mind. My knees weakened, but from a mix of carnal and physical hunger. My body swayed.

He surged forward, placed a hand on my shoulder, and steadied me. Whatever internal battle had warred smoothed along with his expression. "This will not do. Come with me." He reached for my hand, but I tugged it away. I couldn't touch him with these lusty thoughts in my head and continue to respect him.

"And where are you taking me?" My lips flattened into a thin line.

He tucked his empty hands into his pockets. "To my home. I'll make you lunch. I can't have you fainting here on the streets now, can I?"

My brows shot to my hairline. Could I resist falling into my siren way if we were in his house? If so, dining alone in his home felt oddly intimate for acquaintances. Yet the idea of heading to my apartment to the paltry meal, or worse, the grocers to restock my cupboards, seemed like an insurmountable task. I chewed my lip. A beat passed between us, and against my better judgment, my starvation won.

I smoothed my hands over my trousers, forcing a nonchalant demeanor despite the magnitude of this moment. "Luckily, I have you to care for my needs, then."

He snorted. "Sadly, I can only feed you. Do you have the energy to walk, or will I have to carry you?"

A shiver crawled along my spine at the idea of being pressed against his body. Our eyes locked, and an attraction sizzled between us.

Unwilling to push my limits, I squared my shoulders. "I can walk."

I sauntered south through the perpetual layer of snow covering the sidewalks. He rushed behind me, kicking up slush, then matched my stride.

"Do you even know where I live?"

A smirk tugged on my lips. As the herbalist, I knew where everyone in the village lived, having dropped a remedy off at least once at each household. "Of course, with your parents."

He let out a chuckle. "Well, you are at least heading in the right direction, but no, I bought Mr. Rickman's farm two years ago."

My brain hitched as memories of the man with terrible gout popped into my mind. He'd moved and settled in one of the farms between Daviel and Presspin with his daughter and her husband. "I'd heard he sold his parcel but didn't realize it was to you."

"I bought it for Ingrid and myself." He shrugged.

We pressed through the square, past the frozen water fountain, and followed the path lined with two-story stone buildings. This morning, there had been a break between storms, and the usually hunkered-down townsfolk milled about. The passing onlookers gawked at us and whispered amongst themselves. I clenched my fists, certain the daily lunches we'd shared had spurred on gossip. Mateo was a beloved figure, grieving for his childhood sweetheart, while I was considered the village harlot, tolerated because of my skills as an herbalist. Yet Mateo remained unbothered. Instead, he chatted on about Ingrid, telling a story about when he first tried cooking for her and nearly burned the house down.

I chuckled when he got to the point of dousing the burnt chicken with water after having stoked the fire too vigorously. He grinned at my amusement, but a sadness dwelled in the depths of his hazel eyes. Despite the pain, he continued the tale. For the dozenth time since we'd begun our lunches, I wondered how the man could bear speaking of her. However, he often told stories of their childhood spent romping in the woods or musings of their adolescence. Somehow, he'd found a way to balance his grief with life. I admired him for that.

Minutes later, we veered toward the southern outskirts of the town, where the agricultural sector lay. Dark clouds loomed in the distance and would soon converge north. Fortunately, streaks of sunshine warmed the thick layers of snow in this respite between storms. The sweet winter scent lingered in the air, burning my lungs with each step forward.

As we weaved through the cozy homes nestled on farms, Mateo switched the conversation from his deceased betrothed and onto the different crops each farmer yielded as we passed their parcels. I interjected with my knowledge about plant life and herbal properties. The in-depth conversation helped me forget about my hunger and longings. Hadn't this been why I showed up at the Owl's Nest every day? For this easy companionship? Time breezed by, and before I realized it, we'd arrived at his home.

As we reached the farmhouse, my mind hitched. The once ramshackle two-story wooden building now bore a fresh coat of buttercream paint with a whitewashed trim. Rays reflected off the chipper color, giving it a homey aura amongst the icy white world. On the other side lay the acres he would plant. To the right was his parents' parcel.

As I stood, gaping, Mateo increased his pace and entered. He shrugged off his gray coat and hung it on a brass hook. The cotton tunic he wore melded to his lean frame. I licked my lips.

"Are you going to stand there gawking all day, or are you coming in?" He gestured, unaware that my momentary pause wasn't because of the renovations.

Quickly, I approached the patio and tiptoed up the once rickety steps that no longer creaked.

I closed the door behind me and paused in shock. The tiny foyer shone with natural light through the window overhead, causing the polished old oak floors to sparkle. He'd even removed the peeling wallpaper and replaced it with a soft cream paint. Stunned, I turned left, toward the kitchen, curious about what other improvements Mateo had made.

The once cramped kitchen overflowing with Mr. Rickman's treasured newspapers and trinkets now felt spacious. Shelves lined the walls, stacked with dinnerware and hanging copper pans. The scents of sage and mint wafted in the air. A line of potted plants sat on the garden window above the deep-set ceramic basin.

"My gods, you are more domesticated than I am. Aren't you a bachelor? Where are the piles of gin bottles and ashtrays?"

"You can thank my mother. The woman would throttle me if she set foot inside a dirty house. She made it clear that I was to be my own keeper, because my pa is a bit of a messy fellow." He beamed with pride, then turned toward a walk-in larder nestled in the corner of the tidy space.

"Your father and I are the same." I leaned against the wall and crossed my arms over my chest, uncertain of how to act. I couldn't play the seductress and remain unentangled. I didn't know how to interact without slipping into the role of the siren, herbalist, or truth-speaking confidant. Here, I was simply Brielle, and for some reason, the realization unsettled me.

Sensing my unusual awkwardness, he glanced over his shoulder. "You can sit there. You must be exhausted, and please don't feign fainting so I'll carry you to my bed. Even I'm unsure I can withstand that level of temptation."

Despite his jesting, did a kernel of truth lay within the statement? Unable to stop myself, I crooned, "Maybe I should stand, then. I'll swoon, then you can ravish me."

His body went taut as a bowstring. Had I pushed too hard?

He turned to me, and his eyes darkened. "Brielle, if I ever have the pleasure of entangling with you, it won't be a quick romp. I'll keep you in my room for days."

A flush crawled over my skin, and a sense of lightheadedness made the world slant. How did this man have this much of an effect on my body? Fortunately, my empty belly twisted, dampening the amorous feelings. Perhaps I did need to sit down.

A fog began to coat my mind, hazing the world, making it difficult to speak. To my relief, Mateo didn't force conversation. Instead, he sifted through items in the cabinet. He moved with graceful precision, filling a small woven basket with onions, potatoes, and some sort of salted meat wrapped in a cheese-cloth. With his ingredients in hand, he shuffled to the counter facing the window. Sunshine broke through the clouds, warming the space and this peaceful moment. My gaze followed him as he plucked a knife from an oak drawer with a metal handle, laid out the components on the butcher block, and began chopping. He whistled a plucky tune. I leaned my back against the wall, taking in the domestic scene. Despite the silence between us, the moment felt comfortable, like we'd done this many times.

Minutes later, with his ingredients prepared, Mateo reached for a copper skillet hooked on the wall, then placed it on the wood stove in the kitchen's corner. He chucked the meat into the pan. The fat crackled, and the salty aroma filled the air.

As the scent rose, the warmth of a home long forgotten wrapped around me like a beloved blanket. I shut my eyes, feeling the dregs of the long morning pulling me under. As the delicious fragrance heightened, my mind drifted between consciousness and dreams, and a long-lost memory of my father pressed forward. He stood over a woodstove, frying corned beef in a cast-iron skillet. I sat perched on the table, watching with rapt fascination as he mixed the ingredients together. A wide grin spread across his face, causing the deep lines to burrow into his brow. Gray speckled his amber hair, and I could almost feel the warmth exuding from him as he prepared dinner.

"Did I lull you to sleep with my whistling?" Mateo asked, pulling me back to the present.

I blinked, taking him in, cooking for me just as my father had. He stirred the contents that seemed near completion. I'd been drifting toward slumber for longer than I'd realized.

"Is that hash?" My question came out a whisper. How had this meal unlocked such a deeply buried memory?

"You have a good nose." He turned toward me with a smirk, but as he studied me, his features softened.

I could remain silent, but something about Mateo disarmed me. His gaze urged me to speak further. "It was my favorite meal as a child. My father used to make it for me. He was a butcher in the slums of Hallowhaven. He'd fry up whatever cuts of beef we had left when the shop closed. Hash was his specialty."

Mateo lowered the wooden spoon to the pan, and his expression remained smooth, despite this being the first piece of my past I'd shared. "He sounds like a nice man. Does he still live in Hallowhaven?"

A frown tugged at my lips. "No, he died in a carriage accident when I was four. My mother passed away during childbirth. I have no relatives or siblings. After he died, a constable took me to the Aralian temple, where I lived as their ward until..." I fiddled with the edge of my braid, uncomfortable with the vulnerability. I didn't have the strength to discuss Wren and settled on a half-truth. "I left and came here."

To my relief, Mateo returned his focus to the pan. My shoulders slumped as I unburdened these feelings I'd been holding for years. To my surprise, it wasn't an unpleasant sensation.

"That must have been difficult." Mateo reached toward an overhead shelf brimming with dinnerware. He retrieved two porcelain plates and lowered them to the wooden block with a clink.

"I managed." Yet the word tasted bitter. My life had been a game of survival, one I'd played well enough to keep myself alive, but not Wren.

"Of course you did." His words were like a soft caress.

He scooped heaping servings of hash onto the plates, then speared a fork into each mound. With the plate in hand, he spun to face me. Yet he didn't wear that chipper expression. Instead, a seriousness crossed over his countenance.

"You're strong, but you don't have to do everything alone. If you need anything, I'm here. You can rely on me."

For a heartbeat, I fantasized about the loveliness of this scene, imagined it could be my life. What would it be like to come home every day to a warm meal, a listening ear, and a gentle smile? A piece of my heart melted. How had this man penetrated through my layers so quickly? And what would Wren think of this fleeting daydream?

"Shall we?" Unaware of my distress, he gestured to the open doorway, where the formal dining room sat as a bridge between the kitchen and sitting area.

Too famished to flee, I stood and followed him, uncertain of how a simple meal with a friend had turned into such an emotional endeavor.

CHAPTER 5

BRIELLE

As I stepped through the foyer, a gloom settled upon me, cluning to the air in Belmont Manor. For a heartbeat, the morose mood gave me pause. Perhaps I shouldn't have forgone my lunch with Mateo this afternoon. Yet Arianna's summons that I'd join her for tea seemed like the perfect excuse to evade the man who'd crested my emotional barricade so easily the day prior.

"This way." Mrs. Potter gestured for me to follow her, tugging my focus away from Mateo and back to the present.

My boots echoed through the dense quiet as I followed the uncharacteristically mute matron, who guided me without so much as a quick quip. We turned down the long hall, the lush carpets further dampening the sound, as if we walked through a crypt. The past month had brought about many changes to the estate from Lord Belmont's bout of unconsciousness, Beatrix's return, a new ward in Naomi, and an impending funeral for the late Mrs. Park. Given the situation, I didn't prod the woman. When we reached the sitting room, the stern house-keeper opened the door.

"My lady, Ms. Brielle has arrived. Though I have no clue why you'd choose your husband's former mistress as a companion." She gestured toward me with flagrant frustration as we lingered in the doorway.

My lips pursed. Whatever unspoken truce we'd shared while tending to the ailing in the manor had been revoked. Irritated that I had not pestered the matron sooner, I skirted around her, pushing my way into the space.

Instead of joining Arianna on the sofa, I spun to the maid, addressing her directly with a purr. "Didn't you hear? I've been without a paramour and am considering opening my bed to couples. Obviously, Arianna and Silas are at the top of my list. Perhaps I'll be joining them for a far more delicious afternoon delight."

Mrs. Potter's mouth hung agape. She shuddered with rage, and even the sprigs of her icy hair, which had popped from her chignon, seemed to coil at the statement. Maybe coming here had been a wise decision. The woman was quite entertaining when she was flustered.

Her glare bore into me with a wild fury. "My lady would never...my lord would never...and you...and..."

Arianna rushed toward us in a flash. As she reached Mrs. Potter, she laid a gentle hand on her shoulder, soothing her. "Brielle's teasing. Besides, you should rest. You've been running yourself ragged preparing for my mother's remembrance ceremony. I can serve the refreshments."

Tenderness filled the housekeeper's countenance as she took in her lady. "All right, but if she causes you any trouble, you do what you must."

"Brielle won't cause havoc," Arianna said.

"Yes, or Lady Belmont will punish me severely. I do enjoy a good spanking." I winked at Mrs. Potter, then breezed past Arianna.

The housekeeper huffed in frustration, and the sound was followed by Arianna's soothing whispers. I ignored the pair behind me, focusing on the drab space housing two beige couches with a low serving table between them. The wallpaper and carpets possessed the same muted hue, making the formal area devoid of personality. The room had little appeal, yet my stomach grumbled over the three-tiered silver tray brimming with decadent desserts. I licked my lips, salivating over the sugar-coated lemon squares. I reached for the treat, plucked it from the tower, and popped it into my mouth. The tangy sweet taste melted away any worries over this unexpected invitation.

The door clicked closed, and the swishing of skirts fluttered behind me. "Must you be so cavalier? She just started calling you Brielle instead of *that harlot.*"

I spun to Arianna but couldn't argue. Not with the sticky confection coating my tongue.

"Good, you're unable to talk." She crossed her arms over her chest. "Did you forget that I'm a jealous woman? Never mention being in bed with my husband again. Even if it's as a joke." Her irises flashed from blue to black, then returned to blue.

I held up my hands in surrender. "All right, I'll behave. A spanking is one thing, but charring me is another."

At the comment, whatever bravado Arianna had faded. Her lips tugged into a frown.

Dammit. I knew better. She'd previously divulged the horrific details of what transpired in Daviel and the pain she bore from the lives she'd taken. Even her raven mourning gown denoted the somber tone of the recent weeks. Yet here I was, making a mockery of the serious nature of the situation.

"I'm sorry. Let's start again. It's so nice to see you. Lemon squares. I love citrus-flavored desserts." I grabbed another pastry and shoved it into my mouth, stopping myself from saying anything further.

She rubbed her temples. "Forgive me. My power has been unruly as of late, especially where Silas is concerned."

My gaze flicked to the oversized onyx ring on her thumb. She'd lost hers after being kidnapped and imprisoned by her former betrothed's family. We'd been so focused on tending to Silas that I hadn't considered forging her a new band.

I swallowed the sweet treat, then pointed to the loose ring. "Well, that is likely the issue. Come to my shop, and we can recreate a conduit. I'll need to use your power to enchant the stone and set the word-binding spell."

She lowered her hand and blew out a long breath, as if I'd given an answer to the question she'd been pondering. "I'll stop by after the funeral. As of late, I have no energy to spare."

Without waiting for me, she poured herself a cup of tea, then settled on the stiff sofa. Her raven skirts billowed about her, pooling over the bland cushions. She curled into the corner, akin to a black cat ready to nap.

I served myself the steaming chamomile, then sank into the opposite end of the divan. We sipped the beverages in stilted silence. Moments later, she slid the saucer set to the tray, having barely touched the brew. Still lost in her own world, she resettled on the couch and rested her head on the back edge. She closed her eyes. Would she indeed fall asleep instead of divulging why I was here? Did she truly just desire my company? I shook my head, pushing the thought away. Yet in our weeks together tending to Silas, we had bridged the gap from enemies to friends of some sort.

Why had she summoned me? Was she ill? In the quiet, I assessed her as an herbalist. Dark bags lined her eyes, tension tugged around her mouth, and her ethereal features had sharpened. Did she lack adequate nutrition? Even her fair complexion had paled significantly. Despite a pile of treats before her, she'd forgone the pastries.

I lowered my cup to the table, searching through the possible maladies. Head colds had been running rampant. However, her symptoms didn't match. What ailment could be plaguing her that she'd be hesitant to share with me? Lightning flashed through my mind. Her condition was obvious. Kesere had been a little over a month prior. The pieces fell into place like a jigsaw puzzle coming together.

"You're with child!"

She jolted to sitting, her spine going ramrod straight. Pain washed over her countenance so deep it nearly broke me.

"No. I'm not." She shook her head, her loose curls swaying at the motion.

"And you're certain?" I pressed. Given her lack of appetite, her mood swings, and fatigue, she could be pregnant.

"My courses completed three days ago." She folded her hands on her lap and stared at her fingers. "I'm fine. I just can't sleep." She leaned deeper into the settee, as if the stiff cushions would lull her into a much-needed respite.

Understanding washed over me. Nightmares were common for those who went through traumatic events. "Perhaps you need a stronger elixir to—"

"No. I won't be trapped in my dreams. I don't want to remember what happened. What I did." She fiddled with the oversized ring, spinning it in circles.

A tense silence stretched over us. Uncertain of how to comfort her, I stood and searched for the one thing that would provide relief—a drink. To my fortune, a gilded beverage cart sat in the corner, hidden behind a sturdy antique desk. A meager selection of too-sweet sherry and aged cognac lay on the shelf. Selecting the stronger of the spirits, my thumb uncorked the top. My nose wrinkled at the pungent tang emanating from the bottle. I pulled two snifters from the bottom shelf and poured a finger into each. With the beverages in hand, I sauntered to Arianna and thrust the glass forward.

She took the glass and peered into it. "With my power being so untethered, should I?"

"Drink up. Herbalist's orders. Besides, this is barely strong enough to dull some of the ache you carry."

She nodded, placed the rim to her lips, and sipped the contents. She coughed at the potent spirits, and I resisted the urge to chuckle at her naïve nature. Instead, I settled beside her, and we imbibed.

Three drinks later, she sprawled over the couch, practically melting into it. With her more pliant and her health not being her reason for this meeting, I broached the subject of the summons. "Given my busy schedule, why did you request an audience with me, my lady?"

She took another swig of the beverage. "I hate when you call me that."

Ignoring her protest, I continued, "Well, my lady, I'm assuming you didn't request my presence for the sheer pleasure of my company."

"Of course not. If I wanted a lovely tea service, I would have invited Layla or Beatrix." She gave me a watery smile, returning a bit of the fire I'd seen before the incident.

Her expression pinched. "It's Naomi. She hasn't spoken to anyone in days. I've tried. Gods above, I've sat there for hours, hoping she'd say something, anything. She just stares out the window or mills about the abandoned conservatory."

"And what do you think I can do about your sullen sister?" I downed the remaining contents of my glass, sensing this visit had taken a tedious turn.

"She spoke with you when you were here, correct?" Curiosity washed over her features.

"A bit. She asked about the elements in the sleeping potion." I lowered the empty cup to the table.

"That is more than she's said to me since she arrived. Neither Layla nor Beatrix could coax her into speaking. I'm afraid for her. She barely eats, and she sleeps the day away. She's struggling, and I don't know what to do." Her fingers trailed over the etched lines of her snifter.

My fingers pressed into my temples. What was I to do with a grieving girl? Yet after my lunch with Mateo yesterday, memories of my deceased parent lingered in my mind. Despite not divulging much, the familiar twinge of sadness had stayed upon me like a thick cloak. I'd tried my best to shake it, donning my usual siren performance. However, it didn't settle well this morning, making me more susceptible to my emotions than usual.

Sensing my consideration, Arianna stared at me like I was her last hope. My gut twisted, and I gulped down the realization that I cared not only about Silas's well-being, but Arianna's as well. What in the gods' names was happening to me?

I blew out a long breath. "Fine."

Her face brightened. "You will?"

"I will, but first you must finish your cognac, then march straight to bed. You look like death herself." I pointed a finger at her.

"All right. I'll try to get some rest." She squared her shoulders, cocked her head back, and gulped the liquor.

I patted her on the shoulder, impressed by my once sheltered friend. Perhaps she would make a fun drinking partner in the future.

We rose. Arianna swayed, the effects of the alcohol loosening the tightness she carried.

"Do I need to ring for Mrs. Potter or Silas to escort you?"

"No, I'll be fine." She yawned. "Silas is upstairs asleep, anyway. I'll join him in a catnap."

My brow furrowed, and my well buried worries bubbled to the surface. "Are his symptoms getting any better or worse?"

"I'm unsure. It's been nearly a fortnight since he awoke, but I'd expected him to be more virile by now."

My mind hitched on the odd phrasing, then caught on the double meaning. "I see. Well, I can bring a concoction tomorrow to assist with his stamina."

"You will? Thank you!" Relaxed by the alcohol, Arianna tilted her face to me and beamed. Her blue eyes sparkled, and her smile lit up her entire being. Blasts, no wonder Silas had fallen under her compulsion. She'd an oddly disarming charm.

"Come on." I offered her my arm, afraid she might stumble in her drunken state. Together we ventured out of the room, through the hall, and up the stairs.

As we settled on the landing, she untangled from my grasp.

"Sweet dreams, Lady Belmont."

She pouted at me. "I told you to call me Arianna. Ar-i-anna."

A snicker bubbled from me as her inebriated form swayed down the hallway, heading for her suites. With Arianna subdued, I spun in the opposite direction and headed toward Naomi's quarters. I'd visited her room once before, after she'd arrived from Presspin bruised, malnourished, and in shock. My boots padded along the thick carpet, making quick work through the corridor. Though the walls were lined with picturesque scenes and tapestries, my mind remained fixated on the task at hand. My pace slowed as the door came into view. A heartbeat passed as I waited for any sign of life to emit through the thick wood, but no sound came.

Without knocking, I stepped into the dark space. Though it boasted of floor-to-ceiling windows, gray storm clouds loomed, dampening the sunlight. An oversized plush yellow bed sat on the rear wall of the suite, while a floral divan was nestled beside the hearth. Near the sofa sat an untouched lunch tray. Though the room was lovely, nothing noted that the girl occupied the space. No books lined the shelves, nor letters sprawled on the oak desk, nor trinkets on the vanity beside the wardrobe in the corner. The space remained a blank guest room, akin to a waystation for the girl.

Naomi sat stone still, perched on the window seat. Snow flurried against the frost-covered panes. My heels clicked over the wooden floors, but she remained unmoved, staring off into the distance. A familiar pain pressed into my heart. A swell of empathy rose within me for the broken girl. I'd once been trapped in stasis while the world continued on.

Grief clung to her being. Her golden hair laid limply over her shoulder. The faint stinging scent of body odor wafted off her. Had the girl bathed recently? It was unlikely, given the rumpled quality of the plush robe and nightgown she donned. Arianna, Beatrix, and Layla had all tried to get through to her—with kindness and compassion, I was certain. Yet, I sensed a kindred spirit in her and acted as Martha had when she nursed me back to health.

"Get up."

She flicked a watery glance at me, and the sadness in the depths of her gaze nearly gave me pause. I didn't falter.

"Did you lose your hearing in that blast? *Get up.*"

Her nose crinkled in frustration. Her lip twitched in a snarl, and a guttural groan escaped her.

Excellent, a reaction.

"I swear, Naomi Park, when I say get up, that means get up."

She rolled her eyes, and a flare of sheer stubbornness pressed through her depressed aura.

"Get dressed. We are leaving this manor. Presspin isn't much, but it's more amusing than the waterlogged hamlet you called home." A corner of my lip curled in disgust, indicating that the small town were the most ridiculous thing. Hopefully, mocking her beloved home would spark her ire, causing that ember within her to blaze.

"What do you know of Krella?" Her gaze burned with fury; a fire still smoldered within her. Now to add fuel to the blaze.

"I passed through the impoverished waystation. It's nothing but a cluster of broken buildings and rundown farms."

She jolted to standing. Her nostrils flared. Her breaths came in quick, clipped succession. "And what would you know of hardship? Weren't you Silas's whore? I'm sure he set you up with that pretty little shop of yours."

A cackle rattled from me. "Well, he provided me with the funding for my store as an investment, one that's repaid monthly with my proceeds and not my body. Our entanglement didn't occur until much later. Not that it matters. Since you are no longer sulking in the window seat, go scrub yourself clean and get dressed."

She folded her arms over her chest and glared at me. "And why would I do that?"

"Because if we leave the manor for the afternoon, then I can lie to your sister. I'll tell her we had a heartwarming conversation about our feelings. When in truth, we'll have headed to the tavern and grabbed an ale, played darts, and found you...wait you're past your majority, right?"

"My birthday is next month." She stood a little taller and squared her shoulders.

"Close enough. I'll secure you some handsome young chap or pretty chit to flirt with. Once you've crossed into adulthood, I'll find you someone to give your maidenhead to." I clapped my hands. I was sure that come the spring, some chit or chap should also be crossing into adulthood, making them ripe for the picking for the sharp-tongued sister.

"That moment has already come and passed. I'm more experienced than I look." She thrust her hands on her hips.

A beat of silence passed, and her glance drifted as her grief tried to pull her back under its thrall. The fire within her dampened. She turned away, studying the window as if she could see through the snow and into the past. Her voice softened. "I had a life there, in that waterlogged town. I had friends, plans for a job, a lover. It's all gone."

I huffed a sigh and leaned against the wall. "That's true. But now you have two choices. You can wallow about it or rid yourself of these feelings with amusement. Personally, I wouldn't sit here waiting for Mrs. Potter to come barging in to pester me about my lack of hygiene, appetite, and overall state of discontent."

She glanced to the seat, then to me. She pursed her lips in thought. Then her expression smoothed to one of sheer determination. "You'll tell Arianna we had a heart-to-heart, so she'll leave me be?"

"Of course. Wash up and get dressed. I won't take you into town looking like a haggard mess." Before she could answer, I headed for the door to give her privacy.

CHAPTER 6

MATEO

FIONA'S SOFT HUM WEAVED through the tavern, along with the clicking of domino tiles. She swayed to the rhythm of her melancholy melody as she scrubbed a rag over the divots of each glass before placing them into the cupboard below the bar. With the afternoon over, the once lively space sat nearly empty, providing the barmaid the much-needed time to prepare for the bustling evening.

Restless, my fingers thrummed over the smooth wood, creating a staccato rhythm, matching the beat of her tune. As the minutes drummed by, I couldn't help but glance at the bronze clock above the wooden double doors leading to the back kitchen. I should have left a half-hour prior, as the tavern cleared. Now I lingered as the sole patron at the bar while a few straggling elderly men played games at the tables beside the windows.

My restless tapping slowed as my thumb traced over a knot on the sleek mahogany top, swirling along the pattern. But the motion couldn't unravel my jumbling thoughts. I'd been foolish staying, akin to a dog waiting for its owner to arrive home. However, my assumption that Brielle and I would have lunch together hadn't been implausible. After our moment in my home the day prior, I'd thought I'd made some headway. She'd opened up a fraction about her past in Hallowhaven, sharing a story or two about her father when we ate. Yet as a second hour slipped by, I had to acknowledge she might not be coming.

Cheers burst from the men, drawing my attention to them. As Farmer Johnson hooted in victory, my gaze shifted from him and to the window, hoping to see her. But Brielle wasn't sauntering down the sidewalk. Instead, only a thick gloom covered the world.

Disappointed, I lifted my mug and stared at the empty glass. My brow furrowed. It had been my second ale, and a third would be downright foolish. I lowered the cup to the polished bar with a clink. I should venture off and find something else to occupy my thoughts, but my body remained unmoved.

My mind bubbled. Had something changed since yesterday? Though I'd previously suggested we be friends, a fondness had grown between us. Perhaps she would change her mind about allowing me to court her? Yet she longed for a bedfellow. A horrific thought pushed forward. Had she left my home and fallen into the arms of another? Despite having no claim on her, the idea made my stomach churn.

Seconds later, a soft padding of boots clipped behind me against the old wood floor, pulling me from my ruminations. My heartbeat hammered, hopeful it was Brielle sauntering forward, uncaring of her lateness. Maybe her prior day had been filled with maladies and today had been just as hectic, causing her delay? Unwilling to appear eager, my eyes remained on the peeling vintage labels on the gin bottles. The rickety stool to my left scraped over the pine floorboards. The warmth of her body radiated near my shoulder. My pulse raced. Not wanting to appear hurt by her lateness, I settled on a flirtatious gaze and formulated some quick retort that would have her bantering with me, despite her tardiness.

I spun in my seat, knocking knees with the newcomer. My smoldering expression shifted into one of horror at Vincent Gallager's shocked expression. His features shifted quickly to amusement and a bark of laughter escaped the straitlaced man. My shoulders slumped further, curling into myself out of sheer embarrassment.

Seconds later, he stifled his guffawing. "My apologies. I shouldn't laugh, but I wasn't expecting a come-hither look from you or anyone this afternoon."

"I thought you were someone else," I said flatly, trying to hide my embarrassment.

A twitch of a smirk gave away his amusement. "Obviously."

Fiona turned her focus from drying dishes to Vincent, cutting through the awkward moment. "Meat pies to go again?"

He nodded, and the barmaid scurried off to fetch his meal. Instead of reconvening our conversation, he dug into his coat and plucked a polished silver pocket watch. A crease formed between his brow, as if each second of his life needed to be accounted for. As the steward of Belmont Manor, Vincent had little time to socialize. Being two years my senior, we'd spent a fair amount of our childhoods playing together. When he'd reached his adolescence, he left Presspin to apprentice in Hallowhaven with a distant relative to become a steward. Now he often worked ridiculously long hours, which seemed to be taking a toll. Fatigue clung to the lines around his mouth. His usually smooth hair had swooped near his brow, as if he'd spent the morning pushing it back, and heavy bags were highlighted by his round-framed glasses.

"You look run ragged. Are they not feeding you at that fancy manor?" I cocked my head, hoping my tone conveyed my concern.

His features tightened. The wheels seemed to churn in his mind, before he settled on the precise phrase. "It's nothing I can't handle. Lord Belmont's been busy consoling his grieving wife after losing her mother."

"I see." I kept my expression neutral. Gossip had spread like wildfire about Lord Belmont's health. From Vincent's exhausted expression, he'd likely taken on an increased workload, providing the overseer of Presspin time to recuperate.

At the topic of loss, a somber mood permeated the air. Ghosts of our carefree childhoods lingered between us—before he left, back when we were friends instead of mere passing acquaintances. Vincent cleared his throat, cutting through the tension, then returned his watch to his pocket. Thankfully, he shifted the conversation away from death.

"Given the gossip about your daily lunches with Brielle, I'm assuming you've been waiting for her? If so, it might be a while. She was up at the manor this afternoon, having tea with Lady Belmont."

A sense of relief washed over me. She must have been summoned suddenly. My fingers rubbed across my forehead, scrubbing away my thoughts of her with another. Though half the town assumed my desire to pursue Brielle, I didn't want to appear desperate. "We are friends who've met for lunch. Nothing more." Even as the words tumbled from me, my gut twisted.

My lie fell flat. He raised his sharp eyebrow, and disbelief coated his tone. A wry smirk tugged on the corner of his mouth. "Of course."

However, two could play at this game. A suspicion I'd carried for years harkened to the forefront of my mind. A grin stretched across my face. My elbow pressed into the bar, and I leaned my chin on my fist. "I'm sure your long hours at Belmont Manor also have nothing to do with a woman."

A blush crawled over his neck and crested his pale cheeks, melding with his speckling of freckles. Flustered, he choked back whatever emotion he'd felt and sat up straighter in his seat. "Of course not. Lady Beatrix is married and is only in Presspin because of the illness her brother suffered a few weeks ago."

I snorted. "I never mentioned Lady Beatrix, but thank you for affirming my decade-old suspicion."

His mouth worked, trying to form words to speak, but none came. To his fortune, Fiona pressed through the swinging pine doors leading from the kitchen, carrying a burlap sack.

"Three meat pies, and Agnes threw in a few honey buns too." Fiona placed the bag on the polished bar.

Vincent pulled out five Presspin silver and handed them to the barmaid. He grabbed the bag and stood. "Well, I better be off. I need to head back to—"

"Share some of those buns, right?" I winked. All of Presspin knew of Beatrix Belmont's love of the sticky sweet treats.

A sheepish smile tugged on Vincent's lips, then smoothed. With a quick nod, he turned and strode away.

In the silence, a pang of loneliness settled on my shoulders. Over the past year, I'd sequestered myself from the town, focusing on renovating my farmhouse and grieving. I had some connections, but outside of my family, they'd been shared with Ingrid. Yet, since having Brielle over for lunch, I'd realized how small my life had become. She'd filled the once empty space with companionable conversation. Perhaps it was time for me to reconnect with my old friend.

I leapt from my seat and weaved through the tables.

"Wait," I called out.

Vincent slowed his pace, allowing me to catch up.

"I've been thinking maybe I should join you and Liam for a sparring session. You've been begging me to visit this boxing club."

We reached the vestibule bridging the tavern and the inn and paused in front of the reception desk. But the door swung open, cutting our conversation short. A frigid gust hit me as my attention shifted to the newcomers.

My mouth dried as Brielle stood before me, clad in a beautiful green day dress matching the color of her emerald irises. A sensual smirk brushed over her full lips and melted whatever frustration I'd possessed about her tardiness. But the respite didn't last. My jaw ticked as Brielle clung to the arm of a young woman dressed in mourning black.

Vincent flicked a nervous expression to me, mouthed *Lady Belmont's sister*, then spun to the pair. His features smoothed to those of a professional. "Ms. Naomi, it's so nice to see you out and about."

An eerie silence crackled through the foyer as the young woman glared at Vincent menacingly.

His expression flattened. "I'd love to stay and chat, but I must be off. Those ledgers won't balance themselves." Without awaiting a response, he weaved around the pair and darted out the door.

My thoughts swirled, pulling for the rumors I'd heard, that the nineteen-year-old had come with the Belmonts after her mother's death and lives as their ward. Given her age, and the pair's tense attitude toward each other, she wasn't Brielle's new paramour.

Unsure of what to say, I studied Naomi. She resembled Lady Belmont, possessing blond hair, blue eyes, and a similar pale complexion. While Lady Belmont had an ethereal aura with sharp features, this girl had a softness about her cheeks, her lips, and chin.

"Should we continue standing here, or will you introduce yourself?" Brielle thrust her hands on her hips.

"Oh yes, my apologies. I'm Ma—"

"Not you, Mateo. You." She elbowed the young woman in the ribs, who shifted her scowl from me to Brielle.

Brielle cocked an eyebrow, and a silent battle of wills played out between the two women. The younger sighed. "You may call me Ms. Naomi."

"My gods, must you be so formal? You are a farmer's daughter, aren't you? You carry no title, so he, and the rest of the town, shall call you Naomi." Brielle crossed her arms.

"As Lady Belmont's sister, do I not possess an honorific title?"

My hand scrubbed over my face. If they spent the afternoon drinking here, it would end in catastrophe. Brielle's disappearance rankled me, but I couldn't fault her for wanting to assist this girl who was deep within her mourning. She'd a compassionate soul, even if she hid it beneath a flirtatious attitude.

Brielle pivoted to her, eager to fight. "No. You don't. Not when you're acting like a—"

"Ladies." I held up my hands, hoping to cool this sparring match between them. However, Brielle's green eyes twinkled with amusement.

They turned their heated gazes toward me. I gulped at the intensity, but I wouldn't fall to their furies. No, from Brielle's brief mentions of her long-passed father and Naomi's mourning garb, perhaps they needed some comfort.

"Ladies, we could stand here in this dreary place, watching Farmer Johnson thwart his cousins at dominos for the next few hours, or you could come with me. I know of the perfect place to spend an afternoon." I gestured to the door.

CHAPTER 7

FAINT WHISPERS OF SUNLIGHT cut through the clouds, causing the snow to shimmer like gems along the sidewalk. Given last night's storm, a hush had settled over the town, and nary a person traversed the square. To my displeasure, Naomi's grumbling pierced the peaceful silence. I ignored her protest about the frigid weather.

"Just a bit farther," Mateo called out over his shoulder, trying to reassure the girl.

His words didn't soothe her, and perhaps nothing would.

"I wanted to drink my worries away, not trounce through this damn village." She gestured at the two-story buildings made of stone, with their tidy shops on the bottom floor and apartments on the top. Not even the frozen fountain in the square, with its beautiful carvings of torn-apart lovers, swayed her.

"Yes, well, Fiona wouldn't have served you anyway," I lied.

"Then why promise me a drink? Goddess above. Take me home!" she snapped and slowed her pace.

"I'll return you to Belmont Manor once we are done with this outing. Besides, a walk in the fresh air will help your sour constitution." I flicked a glance at her over my shoulder.

Her glare skipped over me and settled on Mateo's back. He squirmed, as if her stare could pierce him.

"And who is he? Your next conquest? Seems a little young. He's easily ten years your junior." She stomped to my side, kicking slush up in her fury.

"He's not a conquest. He's my…" My lips pursed, uncertain of how to classify the man. Yesterday, I'd been far too aware that something had shifted between us as we ate lunch in his home. That cozy scene had flickered a longing within me that was best kept well buried. A beat of silence passed.

She rubbed her gloved fingers together. "Oh, this is interesting. For someone so certain of themselves, you seem quite unsure about him."

When had this mopey girl snapped out of her fog? She pinched her jaw with her thumb and forefinger. Though I didn't care for this change in conversation, at least she was talking. A minute passed, denoted by the crunching of our boots on the snow-covered path.

"What's going on between you two? What am I missing?" The rhetorical questions came from her as she tapped her chin.

I opened my mouth to protest, but the truth hit me to the core. I didn't know how to classify our relationship. The wind whipped flurries about us, softening the stretching silence.

"We meet for lunch every day. That's the detail Brielle is failing to mention," Mateo chimed in with a hint of disappointment.

My nose crinkled. I'd been caught in my manipulation. When Arianna had sent me the last-minute invitation, I'd failed to inform Mateo I'd be missing our daily meal. However, I'd felt too vulnerable after spending the afternoon in his home, opening up about my past. I'd foolishly hoped he would have taken my cut personally, retreated, and ended whatever this bizarre relationship was. However, seeing him in the foyer of the Owl's Nest, I knew he'd been waiting for me, and without anger at my insensitivity. Seeing him had caused a heady sensation to wash over me. After yesterday, I realized we weren't lovers, but we were becoming something more than friends. I should have stayed at the Owl's Nest with Naomi, but I found myself unable to deny his company. For the last few blocks, we walked in strained silence, each of us caught in our own muddling thoughts.

Minutes later, Mateo halted in front of a two-story basalt building. "We're here."

The wooden sign swayed in the breeze, reading *The Artist Alcove*. My brow scrunched in confusion. Naomi took in a sharp inhale as she stared at the windows displaying vibrant compositions. A swell of unshed tears welled in her eyes.

"Why did you bring me here? Arianna told you, didn't she? That I used to sketch." Her jaw trembled, bobbing between rage and sadness.

Mateo pivoted to us and rubbed the nape of his neck. "Actually, this was all my idea. My fiancée passed last year, and this was one of her favorite places. Nellie has a keen ability to help those who are dealing with loss." He shrugged, and his cheerful expression pinched.

I expected her to argue further or stomp off. Surprisingly, she said, "My condolences. Let's get this over with." Then she breezed past him and through the door. The bell chimed, then dampened as the heavy wood swung shut.

"Blasts. Who would have guessed you'd have tamed that shrew?" I blinked at the entrance, in awe that she'd gone in without a fight.

His jaw ticked, and he crossed his arms over his chest, guarding himself. "Sometimes a bit of vulnerability goes a long way."

The double meaning of the statement landed like a punch to the gut. A wash of guilt flooded me and settled on my shoulders. However, I found myself uncomfortable in this stilted silence and wanted to recapture the ease we'd had the day prior. "I'm sorry. I should have told you about my plans to have tea with Lady Belmont."

He huffed a sigh. Then his tense shoulders loosened.

"Shall we stand here all day in this tundra or go in?" I asked before he could say more.

He tugged on the brass knob and held the door open. "After you."

Instantly, a cozy warmth untangled the tightening knot in my chest. I breathed in the scent of charcoal and paint. Naomi had veered to the left, perusing the bucket of brushes, while Mateo strode toward the base of the stairs leading to a loft. My eyes constricted to the bright room, with lamp lights illuminating the walls of paintings. The thick plum-colored carpets softened my footsteps as I approached an art-covered wall filled with watercolors of ripe fruits and picturesque nature scenes.

An acrylic of dancers twirling at the Kesere festival caught my eye, halting me.

"Mateo," a chipper voice called out from overhead. Boots clipped as Nellie burst down the steps. "My gods. Did you come to finish the piece you started over the summer? It's not as bad as you believe. It just needs a little work. Maybe some shading."

The pair embraced, and a niggling pang of jealousy burrowed into my gut. Nellie was a sumptuous thirty-four-year-old widow with bright green eyes, round cheeks, and a luscious mouth. Her curvaceous body was one ancient artists would have immortalized, with full breasts, hips, and thighs. Gods, even I'd craved the woman. Sadly, her tastes were of the male persuasion.

My throat dried as they pulled apart, but Nellie's soft caress remained on Mateo's shoulders. Though she was a dozen years his senior, he seemed to have a taste for older women. Given his interest in me, I should scan these pictures and allow whatever tenderness lived between the two to unfold. The woman's attention darted from Mateo to me. Her smile deepened as she weaved around the man and headed in my direction.

Nellie's chipper rose-color day dress swished beneath her paint-stained apron with each step forward. To my shock, she opened her arms and wrapped me in an embrace. I froze. Sensing my stiffness, she withdrew, providing me space.

"Brielle, it's so good to see you. I was meaning to say hello to you at Kesere, but you left so abruptly with Mateo that I missed my chance. What brings you here?"

My being warmed under her gentle demeanor, and the lightness living within this shop seeped into the marrow of my bones. Under her earnest attention, I couldn't force the sultry siren forward. I turned and pointed to the supplies and the sad girl who perused them. "That's Lady Belmont's sister. She needs some cheering up, and Mateo suggested we bring her here."

"Poor thing. I heard about her mother. How dreadful it must be to lose your parent and home so suddenly. I'll go assist her. Emotions are the perfect breeding ground for art. Mateo, why don't you show Brielle your artwork while I figure out what media is best for Ms. Naomi?" Nellie smoothed her apron, then she strode in the opposite direction, her sable braid swaying with her plucky pace, to cheer the depressed girl.

We stood awkwardly. Luckily, Mateo spoke first. "I'll show you my painting, but you mustn't laugh at my poor attempt."

He gestured to the loft. I arched an eyebrow, curious about why his artwork was stored amongst the owner's treasured items.

Sensing my thoughts, he lifted his hands, showing his palms. "She stores all the unfinished work there."

A witty retort formed, but he shifted from foot to foot. The jest fizzled on my tongue. A heaviness loomed between us caused by an unspoken intimacy as he waited for me to agree to see a part of his soul. I peered at Naomi and Nellie. Staying by the girl's side could serve as an excuse to avoid this blossoming emotional depth, but Naomi's tight features had softened as Nellie showed her acrylic paints tucked within a woven basket perched beside the easels.

My focus returned to Mateo, whose demeanor brimmed with hope. My pulse rose. Something about this moment felt like it would lead me to my doom and further unravel my protective shields. Yet cowardice wasn't my mode of being. Reluctantly, I nodded and followed him up the creaking oak steps.

As we reached the landing, we were accosted by numerous incomplete works leaning against the whitewashed walls. There were at least a dozen in each stack. Unlike the neatly organized main level, this space was chaotic.

"Many of these were Nellie's husband's. I've encouraged her to complete them, but she says their styles are too different." He stepped into the loft and approached a haphazard pile.

I didn't move, unwilling to trespass into the memories of the dead, fearing it was dishonoring them. My fingers gripped the smooth oak banister, and I remained on the landing while he milled through the graveyard of art.

Sunlight crested through a small circular window, washing over Mateo and the many canvases. My mind couldn't focus on these incomplete pieces of scattered colors throughout the room, akin to petals floating through the wind in the spring. Mateo hunched over a stack, his long fingers sorting through the canvas as he searched. His chestnut locks flopped over his forehead, pulling my attention to his sharp cheekbones. He was beautiful, and I'd shamelessly thought of him last night as I brought myself to pleasure. But somehow my longings for him had turned into something more than simple attraction.

At the realization, a sensation burned down my legs, urging me to run. Before I could, Mateo stood with a canvas clutched in his fingertips. "Here it is."

He skirted around the piles of half-finished pieces with his work pressed against his firm chest, hiding the contents.

My pulse climbed. My mouth dried. We were growing too close. Once he showed this part of himself, I wouldn't be able to turn back. Yet as he stood before me, ready to bare his soul, I couldn't move.

The usual confident countenance he wore softened to that of a shy chap. "Don't laugh."

He spun the picture.

A gasp escaped me as I took in his beloved, perched beneath a tree. Light crested through the branches, illuminating the soft features of her face, from her arched nose to her apple cheeks and plump lips. It wasn't an exact likeness, but a depth of emotion lay within each stroke.

A portion of the barriers around my heart shattered. How had he been able to bear painting the love he lost and then have the resolve to show it to me? My well-buried pain had bubbled to the surface yesterday and overwhelmed me now. My lips tightened as I fought a well of emotion clamoring to the surface.

"Oh gods. I didn't realize it was that bad." He tucked it behind a charcoal of a winter wilderness scene, as if it had offended me. He shuffled on his feet, seeming uncertain.

"No...It's beautiful. I can tell how much you loved her." The earnest statement fell from me.

Mateo scrubbed the back of his neck. "I came here after Ingrid died, needing to capture some of her essence. That is when Nellie suggested I paint her. I tried with Nellie's assistance, but I never could quite perfect Ingrid's likeness. It made me realize I couldn't recreate the past. That's when I started to build a new life."

To my horror, a hole in my shields had broken and whispers of emotion oozed out. Untethered, the truth tumbled from my lips. "No one tells you how hard it is to start over once you've lost your beloved."

Mateo's eyebrows shot to his hairline, then lowered. To my relief, he didn't push. A heavy silence settled over us. He shifted his gaze to the ceiling, searching his mind. "Can I show you Ingrid's last sketch?" His features lightened.

Grateful for the change in subject, I nodded. He gestured to the stairs. Silently, we ventured to the main floor.

Instead of heading to the chatting women, who were beside a metal bucket of charcoals, we turned toward the wall of watercolors. But we didn't halt where I'd once stood. Mateo veered left again, into an alcove where black and white sketches embedded in wood frames covered the walls. My feet slowed as I approached the drawing in the center of the display. A small copper plaque with the engraved words: *In Loving Memory of Ingrid Green, friend, daughter, and fiancée.*

I stood ramrod still, staring at my likeness. However, unlike the usual sultry persona, this had captured the parts I'd hidden down within my core. She'd etched a gentleness to my brow, a softness in my gaze, and a sadness in my smile, capturing the pain I tried to hide. Speechless, I studied a version of myself I thought had died with Wren.

"She drew this right before she passed. Do you remember the long afternoons you spent at her bedside? When you'd leave, she'd sketch your features until she grew too weak and the fever delirium set in. I believe working on this kept her alive for a few days longer. She was eager to capture you, the *real* you. At least, that's what she told me. I've admired this portrait a lot over the past year. I've been desperate to see this same gentle expression for myself."

I inched closer to him. My heart thumped. Our mutual longing sizzled in the air, a melding of physical desire and this unfamiliar pang of emotional need swirled within me. Could I reveal this vulnerability to someone who wasn't dying? Did I possess the courage to expose a fraction of what lay beneath my rigid depths?

My logic faltered. How had he disintegrated so much of my protective shell in such a short span of time? "Mateo, I—"

"I'm so sorry, but Ms. Naomi wants to leave…" Nellie glanced between us, and a blush crossed her cheeks. "Oh my, I didn't mean to interrupt."

I shook off my momentary insanity and resecured the protective camouflage. "Mateo was showing me Ingrid's final piece. I'm flattered that she chose me as her final subject." But even as I pointed to the portrait, I couldn't plaster on the siren persona. A pang pierced through my heart like it was restarting.

"I'm beyond honored." I glanced at Mateo, hoping my words conveyed the depth of this feeling that drowned me.

Sensing the shifting mood, Nellie's grin widened as if she'd borne witness to the beginning of something wonderful. "Perhaps we can persuade Naomi to stay for a cup of hot chocolate and some gingerbread? And maybe I can convince her to tell you a bit about her past in Krella. Did you know she planned on apprenticing under the local physician? It seems she may have more in common with you, Brielle, than with me."

CHAPTER 8

BRIELLE

SMOKE BILLOWED FROM THE funeral pyre, casting a gray plume into the fading brilliant purples of dusk. An acrid scent filled the air as the dying flames consumed the note Martha had sent. I blew out a breath and shifted my gaze to Silas, who glowered at the disintegrating page. This day had not gone as I'd suspected. Yesterday, after escorting Naomi back from the The Artist Alcove with a leaflet of pages, charcoals, and a belly filled with gingerbread, I'd assumed I'd crested through the final emergency on the Belmonts' behalf. However, that assumption had been thwarted when a raven landed on my windowsill, carrying that message from my friend. One that issued a warning about the Aralians searching for *Arianna Park*. Though Martha didn't know of my connection to the cursed lady, the note had been one of caution and her fear that eventually the disciples could expand their search to Presspin. I'd waffled between sharing the missive and keeping it to myself as the day dragged on. However, given the urgency of the information, I couldn't keep this secret to myself.

Silence washed over us. I prepared myself for some morose statement or even a sharp outburst. Instead, a horrible hacking cough emitted from him. He withdrew his fingers from his mouth, and horror panged in my gut. Blood. Silas had coughed up blood.

Pain coursed through his amber eyes, conveying the unspoken reality I'd feared since the incident in Daviel. Yet I'd foolishly allowed Arianna's faith to coat me like a child's blanket, wrapping us in a fairy tale. Why had I let hope take root when the truth had been obvious? I'd seen the effects of the wasting sickness that plagued the cursed. Silas had expended enough energy to destroy a battalion of Aralians and an entire estate. He shouldn't have lived to tell the tale. He should have died that day.

Pop.

The smoldering embers broke the heavy moment we were drowning under. His lips pressed into a flat line of dismay. He tugged the handkerchief from his pocket and scrubbed away the crimson staining his fingertips. My mind swam. How had everything changed so quickly? Months ago, we'd been hidden in Presspin, far from the Aralians' reach, and Silas was well. Now they were scouring the territories for Arianna and Silas...

An icy wind howled, breaking my thoughts. Flurries shifted from the snow-covered ground, extinguishing the last whispers of life within the flames, plunging us into darkness. I blinked, adjusting to the pitch-black world with only the faintest light from the crescent moon to illuminate the night.

A watery bark emitted from him, causing a shiver to course down my spine and settle at its base. In the shadows, I could barely make out his frail form hunched over as he fought for oxygen. Yet this fit dislodged me from the swirling emotions and tugged me into my herbalist training. He needed to get out of the cold and beside a fire before a chill settled within him. Concerned, I closed the distance between us and rubbed soothing circles over his back. His muscles constricted beneath my palm. After an agonizingly long minute, he drew in a sharp inhale.

"I must return to Arianna." He straightened, acting like the past few minutes were nothing of note.

"My gods, are we not going to speak of what is happening?" I gritted my teeth and stared at the crimson spittle splattering the snow.

He grunted, but even he couldn't ignore the ailment seizing his body. Silas's usually well-fitted jacket hung loose on him, and he'd easily dropped two stones over the past few weeks. Gray peppered his once raven hair, his features had sharpened, and his skin had taken on a sickly pallor. The once lively thirty-year-old now appeared decades older.

He took a step forward but teetered. Panicked that he would collapse in the slush, I rushed forward and laced my arm with his. Surprisingly, he leaned against me like a crutch instead of fighting my assistance.

"You pig-headed dolt. When did your symptoms begin and why didn't you send for me?" I took his arm, wrapped it over my shoulder, and began walking him down the slick path toward the house.

A bitter chuckle escaped him. "This was the first occurrence. Unfortunately, you were here to bear witness."

I ground my teeth. "And if I hadn't?"

He remained silent beside me, with only his rasping breaths mixing with our boots crunching on the icy path to break the tension. The stubborn man would have hidden this illness until the end. My nostrils flared in frustration. I bit back my retort. This wasn't the time to argue. I could chastise him once he was safely tucked into bed.

To my dismay, his sluggish pace slowed, and he leaned his body more heavily against mine. A wheeze whistled through him. Seconds later, he halted, gasping for air. My temporary ceasefire fizzled, and frustration overruled my concern.

"You should thank the gods I'm here. In the morning, send Grey to my shop. I'll have a concoction to slow the progress of your illness."

He withdrew from me, swaying, but out of sheer stubbornness, he straightened. "What will your tinctures do? Make me comfortable? I'm aware there's no cure."

While training with the Aralian herbalist, I'd witnessed this ailment firsthand. It ate away at the cursed, starting with bouts of fatigue, then respiratory issues with spewing blood, followed by fevers, until their drained bodies succumbed. There was no cure, and the disciples didn't care to concoct one. They viewed the blighted as beneath them, horrid creatures they were tasked with tending to. It wasn't until after I'd escaped them and met Martha that I'd discovered the darker truth. The Aralians were draining the cursed of their power and vitality.

Their energy fueled the weapons they used to subdue them, and this disease was the effect of the power expenditure.

"I'll be lucky if I live to spring, right?" he asked, cutting through my thoughts.

His symptoms were progressing at an alarming rate. Most cursed could go years under the suppression spells while being slowly drained. Yet the spells were akin to a slow stream that the disciples leached through the word-binding wards. But Silas had exploded, expending energy akin to a flood of power bursting through the dam.

"Yes." The word was a soft whisper, laced with disbelief.

He tilted his head back, staring at the stars, knowing the Great Beyond beckoned him. An agonizing silence blanketed us. His brow furrowed, and a swell of anguish rose within me. Though I'd never loved Silas romantically, I was fond of him. Another gust blew, causing goose bumps to raise on my skin. In this stasis, we stood, unwilling to move forward and unable to move backward. But I had to do something. My brain scrambled to concoct a plan, desperate to save my friend. Despite the long-shot, I settled on a course of action. "I can write to Martha. She may know something. She was a fully fledged disciple. Though she wasn't in Delphine's inner circle, she might—"

"No. If you ask about the wasting sickness, she will put two and two together. Everyone believes Arianna caused the explosion at Terrell Estate. Martha will assume it is Arianna who is suffering from this ailment. We can't trust her, not when the Aralians have a bounty on my wife's head. I already risked Arianna's life by not being cautious enough." He ran a hand through his hair, and his shoulders slumped. Defeat coated every inch of him.

I smoothed my tone, trying to hold my frustration at bay. "She's trustworthy. I promise you; she won't betray us."

"And what if she does? Would you risk Arianna's safety? I'm set to die, but Arianna will live. Unless the Aralians find her." His jaw set into a firm line of determination.

A beat of silence washed over us as we lingered at the edge of the garden that had succumbed to the winter. The topiaries were now nothing but snow-covered bushes, and the once beautiful flowers had withered months prior. Now, only the icy white blanketed the world. I chewed the inside of my cheek, wanting to argue but seeing his logic.

"Then we agree?" he asked.

This couldn't be the end for him, yet I'd worked with the healers in the temple and knew of no remedies. Would we risk Arianna on a fool's errand? I needed to process through what to do about this situation.

I approached. "We don't need you freezing to death before your time. Let's go."

Satisfied with my lack of argument. He placed his arm over my shoulder, and we walked the stretch to the house in silence.

The temperatures plummeted with each passing minute. Silas's teeth chattered, and his steps dragged through the slush. I worried I wouldn't be able to pull him to the manor.

Finally, we pushed through the gardens, and the stone estate came into view. Hundreds of candles shone through the windows, lighting our way like a beacon to safe haven. As we reached the front steps, a light sheen of sweat coated my forehead, and I, too, panted from the exertion.

"When will you tell her?" My brows knitted together.

"Give me a few days of letting her believe we are safe and well." He scrubbed a hand over his gaunt face and forced his hunched body to stand.

As if summoned by our conversation, the massive wood doors flung open. Arianna stood in the archway, flooded by the warm candles from the chandelier. She clung to a black shawl, and her weary blue eyes settled upon us.

"There you are. I was about to send Roger to fetch you." Arianna's slippers padded over the salt-covered stone.

"Just moving slower than usual." Silas unraveled from my grasp and reached for his beloved.

The instant they touched, his graying pallor warmed, and his gaunt features plumped. His gaze shone with love as he took in his mate. He brushed a kiss to the top of her head, breathing in her scent as if she could indeed anchor him to this world. Slowly, they traversed the steps, arm in arm, as if nothing could tear them asunder, not even death herself. I remained frozen, drinking in the scene of my two friends who'd soon suffer as I had. I choked down a swell of emotion, unwilling to be undone. I'd give him this week, but if he didn't tell her by then, I'd speak the truth myself.

As they reached the doorway, Arianna halted and spun to me. "Are you coming in? I had Mrs. Potter prepare lemon squares again."

I forced a purr to my voice, hoping to convey ease. "No. I don't want to intrude on your evening, especially after the elixir I gave you."

A blush washed over her cheeks, and Silas cocked an eyebrow at his wife. Though these tonics wouldn't save him, at least I could buy him time with his beloved.

"Come to my shop, and we'll have a chat. Until then, someone fetch Roger to take me home." I pressed my hands to my hips, forcing a confidence I didn't feel.

CHAPTER 9

UNCOMFORTABLE, I SHIFTED IN the plush seat in the sleigh. But every bump down the snow-covered hill caused my already uneasy stomach to slosh. Silas was dying, and Arianna would soon suffer the same fate as me. A life without her mate. At the thought, my nostrils burned with unshed tears. I sniffled them back, blaming the icy gusts blasting over my face. Yet this chill seemed to spread through my soul, freezing me from the inside out. I curled deeper into the plush blanket, hoping that the paltry warmth would soothe me, but it didn't.

My focus shifted onto the winter scene, slipping past me instead of on my long-lost love and doomed friend. The lantern bobbed ahead, lighting the slick path down the slope. Soft flurries tumbled from the dark sky, akin to gems twinkling against black velvet. The aged evergreens swayed under the accumulating pressure of the freshly fallen snow. Yet the night held no charm, only harshness. Even the horses seemed to canter in rhythm with my escalating heartbeat as they pulled the sled, heading for my home. Yet with each agonizingly long minute trapped in this sleigh, my tightly bound emotions swelled like a balloon ready to burst.

When had everything become so complicated? A few months ago, I'd been languishing in lovers, imbibing in whiskey, and keeping the specters haunting me at bay. Now, my tidy life was akin to dominos falling in rapid succession. A sour taste lingered on my tongue, one that needed to be washed away with something far richer than the cheap liquor in my empty cupboards.

"Take me to the Owl's Nest," I shouted over the clopping of the horses' hooves.

I leaned deeper into the seat and closed my eyes, needing a moment away from reality. My attention clung to the ting of metal over the frozen ground mixing with the horses' pants. My limbs grew heavy with the weight of these memories and emergencies. Fatigue dampened the edges of the world. At some point, the dark caverns where my memories lay pulled me under, and the past leapt forward.

I was late again, and Helga would award me with ten lashes for my tardiness. But I didn't care, not as I slunk through the marble hallway, having satiated a much more important need. I licked my lips, still tasting Wren on them. We'd writhed in the wee hours, before the larks sang their warning song. As the morning light crested through her warded windows, I'd slipped away with the patrol none the wiser of my entanglement with the blighted beauty imprisoned in the temple. To my delight, the sleeping tonic I'd drugged the disciple with had kept her slumbering well past the dawn. As I rushed to the medical ward, a flurry of hushed whispers just beyond gave me pause.

My once languid limbs tightened. If they discovered me traipsing these corridors, those guarding this wing would beat me. The punishment would then be followed by days without food. Instinctively, I pressed against the cold stone wall and peeked around the corner, waiting for the coast to clear.

My face fell as I took in Delphine's second-in-command, Zephira, speaking with another Aralian who'd donned a white robe that obscured her features. Tension crawled through me. If I was caught lurking here by an upper disciple, a bashing would be a welcomed punishment. I held my breath.

"At the next full moon celebration, that's when Delphine wants to sacrifice her." Zephira's words were whispered, but her alto tone carried throughout the echoing corridor.

Bile burned in my throat. Which girl, blossoming into her majority, would be subjected to the lecherous needs of the high council now? Delphine had auctioned off my virginity, like all those in her care, once I'd crossed into adulthood. Wisely, I'd set my sights on a handsome son of a high council member. As a virgin himself and not accustomed to the court's proclivities, he allowed me a more palatable experience than most. He'd spent a fortune, and the short-cocked fellow finished quickly.

My feisty spirit didn't call to the ham-fisted ruffians who preferred the sweet-tempered girls who lacked the foresight to concoct a plan to give them a modicum of control. Many of them wept for weeks. If I found out the name of the maiden, I could slip her a tonic to blur her mind into a hazy, horrible dream. This was the price we orphan girls paid for our years of room and board. Those who shirked their debt were slaughtered before the remaining youth. We all learned that crossing the Aralians meant death, but I could help this girl in my own way. Determined, I tiptoed to the corner.

"It's time. Delphine believes Wren is the strongest..."

My ears buzzed, muddling their words. My pulse rose. The world tilted as if I'd stepped into a horrid, foggy nightmare. Wren. I'd always wondered why they had her confined within our walls when no other blighted was bound here. There had been rumors that her curse had been too strong to contain with simple wards, requiring her to be in our continuous care to keep her deadly power at bay. I'd believed the lie. At twenty-seven, she'd shown no signs of the wasting sickness, where other cursed would have already begun withering. Instead, her violet eyes shone with unbridled energy, as they had when she stepped into the temple a year prior. Yet I should have suspected a far more nefarious fate for my love. I forced my mind to steady and listened, but I only heard the click of heels over the marble floor. I'd missed whatever they'd said while I panicked. The padding of their steps headed away from me, but dread permeated my bones anyway. Wren was in danger. I would save my beloved or die trying.

The carriage lurched to a stop, jarring me from the past and plunging me into the present. I wobbled, nearly falling from the seat. Disoriented, I scoured the scene. My soul expected to see the temple I'd once called home. Instead, the familiar two-story stone building lay before me. The sense of solace I'd hoped for never came. Only this hollow emptiness had been my constant companion since losing Wren. But this tavern held the key to numb my worries with a drink. Roger shifted, ready to leap to my assistance. Before he could aid me in my exit, I unfurled myself from the blankets and scooted off the seat.

"Best be on your way. I'm sure Hannah is waiting for you." I fluttered a quick wave, shooing him.

The footman didn't question me. He flicked the reins, and the sleigh slid down the street.

I pushed the door open, and warmth enveloped me. My boots clipped along the pine floors, past the reception desk and toward the tavern. Raucous laughter accosted me, jolting me from the once gothic scene and into a dreamy sepia hued world. Unaware of my agony, men blustered about, chatting over frivolities as they drank ale at the round tables. The group of elderly farmers had switched from dominos to cards. Mr. Johnson grinned, unwilling to be outmatched in this game either. Despite my better judgment, my gaze flicked through the scene for the man who kept trying to restart my broken heart, because his cheer could cut through the gloom. The second the thought entered my mind, I halted. A flush washed over my skin. Had I subconsciously come here to seek him out? I was growing too close to him.

Mateo wasn't here, but my brain hitched at an oddity—Rosalind Collins imbibing at the bar. Given my jumbled feelings, a row with my nemesis might numb the ache. Foolishly, I headed to her and perched on the stool next to hers.

A few seconds passed. Perhaps she was unaware of my presence. She stared at couples playing darts with a wistful expression coating her features. A melancholy aura hung about her, but the usually tightly wound woman's countenance had loosened. Her typically scrunched shoulders had lowered to a limp slope. Her pale blond locks cascaded down her back, and she donned rouge, softening her frigid complexion. Given her odd mood, perhaps I shouldn't unleash my frustration on this woman sipping her sparkling wine. But she broke this calm moment when she whipped her saddened gaze to me.

"Come to gloat?" She lowered the flute to the mahogany counter and spun toward me, nearly knocking her knees with mine.

I arched an eyebrow, having no idea what the woman was speaking of. I'd spent most of the day tending to ailing families, then I'd gone straight to Belmont Manor for the funeral. "Gloat?"

"Stop playing the fool. The whole town has heard that Corina is pregnant with my husband's baby. Well, he's not my spouse anymore. He'll wed my once best friend, and they'll make such a sweet little family." Bitterness laced her tone.

She picked up the flute, kicked her head back, and downed the contents. "He was right. I was the problem." Her fingers traced along a knot on the polished wood, and her shoulders slumped further.

I'd wondered if they'd had fertility issues. She'd never requested an elixir and hadn't borne a child. An awkwardness settled between us, heightened by the gossiping chits chatting behind me about the abandoned woman.

"Whiskey?" Fiona called out from my right as she pivoted her attention from the gossiping gaggle to me.

I gave a curt nod. She grabbed a snifter and poured two fingers of the amber liquor, then slid it to me. "It's on the house for the headache powder you gave me."

Rosalind tapped her nail against her flute as a man at the other end of the bar shouted for Fiona's attention. The barmaid shuffled away without another word.

"Look how low I've sunk, with only you to keep me company. And the tavern wench didn't even refill my wine." Rosalind tapped a nail against the empty crystal. Her mouth puckered into a pout.

Exhausted, I lifted the glass and drained it in one gulp. "Happy now?"

To my shock, she let out an uncouth snort. "Of course not. I'm a barren, aged spinster that not even the ugliest man in town wants. All those years wasted."

I cocked my head, taking in this new side of Rosalind Collins. This evening, her manicured persona had fractured, showing this almost likable raw version. She seemed to have changed her dress, replacing her matronly attire with a low-cut gown displaying her apple-sized breasts. The deep plum hue on her lips made her faint complexion creamy. Sensing my thoughts, her icy gaze widened, and she leaned closer, leaving inches between us. Her strawberry and wine breath washed over me.

"Maybe someone desires me? Even if for one night?" She reached for me, and her hand caressed my cheek. A yearning mixed with pleading lived in her eyes.

Her face brimmed with unsatiated lust. I'd been correct in my guess at the Kesere festival. She did want me. We loathed each other, yet wouldn't she make the perfect bedfellow? Wouldn't coupling with her send Mateo the ultimate message, that I could never care for him? With Rosalind, there would be nothing but meaningless sex. Our hatred would fuel our passion, bringing our releases to new heights. I could lose myself and bury these emotions while entangled with the body of my enemy. Wasn't this exactly what I'd been wanting for weeks? Yet something recoiled within me.

Sensing my hesitation, she lowered her hand to my neck, trailing a lazy finger along the slope. "The village has been whispering about Mateo's vow. He wants what we all know you can't give him—love. Let him go. Perhaps he'll connect with Lady Belmont's sister, and they can start a new life together. And you..." Her lips hitched into a smile. "I can provide you what you need, pleasure with no attachments for as long as you'd like."

CHAPTER 10

MATEO

I WINCED AS THE cold air rushed into my sore nostrils. The twinge of coppery tang lingered, mixing with the sweet earthen scent. Instinctually, I rubbed a gloved finger over my battered nose, certain a bruise would blossom. However, what had I expected would happen when I stepped into the boxing club? That I would sit and be entertained? Instead, Liam had tugged me into the ring, stripped me of my coat, and challenged me to a round to assess my fighting stance. To my dismay, he'd knocked me off my feet within minutes. Blood had trickled down my face, coating the chalk-covered floor, ending our brief bout. This caused the hulking owner to take pity on my lack of skill, promising a pint to soothe my wounded pride.

A gust blew through my thick wool jacket as the temperature plummeted. I shifted from one foot to the other, attempting to stay warm as Liam locked the door. The jingling of keys echoed through the silent evening, followed by the clomping of boots behind me.

"Don't sulk." Liam clapped a heavy hand on my back, almost jostling me to the ground. "Come on. Let's have that drink."

I flicked a sidelong glance at the man. He towered over me, being a head taller and four stones heavier. Yet a genuine warmth radiated from his chestnut eyes. Though I knew him by reputation, we hadn't spoken much, given our fifteen-year age difference. While occasionally, I felt like a youth clamoring toward manhood, he'd established himself years prior, touting a husband, a home, and a beloved business.

"Let's make it two pints. One for each black eye I'll be sporting in the morning." I strolled forward, cresting from under the awning shading the entrance and onto the snowy street.

Liam strode in step beside me. "I'm sure Ms. Brielle has a poultice to help with that." He gave a knowing grin, which highlighted his dark tan skin.

My mouth dried at the mere mention of the red-haired beauty. A day ago, I'd shown her Ingrid's last drawing, and in doing so, revealed a piece of my soul. When we had refreshments with Nellie, Brielle had redirected her attention to Naomi, avoiding our emotionally charged moment. Then her abrupt absence today gave me pause. I'd hoped she was indeed too busy to meet, given the ailing families and the funeral for Lady Belmont's mother. She'd at least sent a note with Fiona notifying me of her absence for our daily meal. But my doubts about our burgeoning connection had led me to leave my house and seek a diversion.

"Why are you so pensive?" Liam's voice boomed through my ruminations.

My gaze shifted from the icy path leading toward the square to the man who watched me with a furrowed brow.

"It's nothing." I shoved my hands into my pockets, focusing on the footprints scattered through the slush, avoiding his penetrating stare.

"I understand. It's far easier for men to beat the tar out of each other in a round of fisticuffs than discuss the inner workings of their minds."

I flinched at the accuracy of the statement but allowed the stretch of silence to loom over us. Snowflakes flurried about, further insulating the world. We wove past the neatly lined stone buildings highlighted by the lamplights. My fingers scrubbed my nape. As seconds ticked by, I couldn't shake his curious regard.

"It's Brielle. She's enamored me for months. I think she's beginning to see me as more than a friend, but I fear I'm nothing more than some simpering puppy amusing her while she waits for someone else."

We passed the frost-covered fountain silently, the sounds of the night dampened by the falling snow encasing the village. Lights flickered on the tops of the two-story buildings, where families were nestled inside their cozy dwellings. For a heartbeat, I pictured my home, and for once, a thought of cooking for Brielle replaced my usual memories of Ingrid. A watery smile tugged at the corners of my lips.

Sensing my musings, Liam scrubbed his stubbled chin, then broke the silence. "I understand your impatience. I was smitten with Dante. While he was uncertain. I wanted to push him into a relationship before he was ready. But my mother, gods bless her, told me to give him time to realize his affection for me. After months, he succumbed to what I hoped lived between us and declared his love. We've been inseparable ever since. If Brielle does care for you, allow her the space to reveal her feelings in her own time. Be patient."

I nodded. I'd prodded Brielle enough, showing her part of the reason why she captivated me. Now I should wait for her to reciprocate.

"How did you and Dante meet?"

Fortunately, Liam took the bait and switched the topic away from the vivacious vixen and onto his husband.

We chatted for the remaining minutes, and our conversations filled the quiet evening devoid of townspeople. A few blocks later, we reached the tavern. Lights flickered through the windows, casting a gentle glow over the dark night. As we reached the entrance, the door swung open, and Brielle emerged, milliseconds from careening straight into me.

Her green eyes locked on to mine, and she shuddered with fury. I stepped back, reeling from her sudden appearance and unbridled rage. Had we planned on meeting here after the funeral?

Sensing the bubbling tension, Liam slipped past her and into the establishment. Cheers spilled out of the tavern, then muted as the heavy wood door closed behind him.

"What's wrong? Were we supposed to meet tonight?" My hand scrubbed over my brow.

Her shoulders rose and fell with clipped breaths, causing the velvet raven mourning dress to strain across her chest. Her usually braided tresses were woven into an intricate chignon, and a coquettish blush colored her cheeks.

"We weren't." She brushed past me and stormed off in the opposite direction.

I blinked, flummoxed. I shook off the haze and sprinted down the slick sidewalk after her. She quickened her pace, but she couldn't outrun me.

"Wait! What's the matter?" My hand landed on her shoulder, anchoring her to the spot.

She twirled to me with frustration burning in her gaze. "Gods above, everything is wrong. I could've been free from these feelings. But I said no!" Her tone softened to disbelief. "Why did I say no?"

Her body rattled, as she tried desperately to contain her emotions. My brain grappled, trying to understand her jumbled statements. Then, to my shock, her eyes welled with tears, giving me pause. Her breaths quickened, and she trembled. I feared she'd break into a million pieces. Concerned, I closed the distance between us and tugged her into my embrace, hoping I could hold her together. Something had unsettled the strong-willed woman, causing chinks to form in her thick armor.

Agitated, she pummeled her fists against my chest, unwilling to accept my comfort. But with each blow, her anger capitulated to her melancholy.

An exhausted sob escaped her, followed by short sniffles. Finally succumbing to her suppressed sentiments, she leaned her forehead into my shoulder, and her tears seeped into my collar.

My heart pounded, counting the passing heartbeats with her wrapped in my arms. We stood on the abandoned sidewalk, nestled between the closed florist and butcher shops. The snow washed over us, cleansing us. Desperate to provide comfort, I stroked along her back, hoping to give her a fraction of my strength. Time slowed. Eventually, she stifled her soft cries, then her once pliant body stiffened.

I loosened my grasp around her waist, allowing her the ability to free herself. Mortified, she withdrew from me.

"It's all right. You can cry. I won't tell anyone." I held up my hands, showing my palms.

Her features pinched into an adorably flustered expression. "Blasts, I'm a damned watering pot." She wiped the moisture from her cheeks with her gloved thumb.

I cleared my throat. "Nobody would dare accuse you of being a whimpering woman. Tell me what caused this."

She smoothed her hands over her black mourning dress, as if the action could also unfurl her emotions. She paused. Her features tightened as her attention turned to me. "It's Silas."

She scanned the empty street, making sure it was indeed devoid of listeners.

"It's complications from the pneumonia. He's getting worse. He's dying, and there's no cure," she whispered, each word straining in her voice.

My palm cupped her cheek. "I'm so sorry."

She leaned into my touch, breathing me in. "I've already lost so many people. My father, my beloved, and now my friend. I don't have the strength to lose anyone else."

The double meaning burned into my soul as her features softened, conveying a deeper well of affection than she admitted.

"Kiss me. I can't dwell on this anymore. I just want to be free for a moment," she whispered.

I held her gaze. Did she not realize what she was asking? I burned with passion for her. She'd plagued my dreams and my waking moments. Her luscious form had blazed in my thoughts when I found self-release. A part of me worried that if I allowed myself even an innocent peck, I'd be driven mad with longing and I would take her against the brick building. But how could I deny her this simple request?

My pulse surged as my lips brushed against hers. My tongue traced along the seam of her mouth, tasting the tang of whiskey. Instantly, she deepened the connection, wrapping her arms around my neck. She devoured me as if I could satiate her agony. Lightning shot through my veins, heating my blood and pooling into my groin. My eager cock twitched, wanting more of her. Drunk on desire, my fingers skated from her waist to the lush curve of her hips. I drew her closer. A desperate yearning boiled, and I feared this mere sensation would have me bursting within moments. The year of celibacy had come to a boiling point, pushing my urges beyond my logic. I stepped forward, melding my body against hers.

To my shock, she pressed a palm to my pectoral and pushed me away. I gaped, surprised, as she stumbled back. Despite her lusty stare, she set her jaw into a hard line of determination. "Stop. I respect you too much for you to break your vow like this. Let's leave it at a kiss."

Liam's words echoed through my mind—*be patient*—halting my argument. We both needed time to discover the depth of our affection for each other. A strained tug against my breeches clouded my judgment, making me hungry for another moment before we parted. I inched closer.

She held up her hands. "No. I won't be able to stop myself again. I'm going home. Alone. I'll see you tomorrow."

Without awaiting my answer, she pivoted and briskly walked away.

I forced myself to remain rooted to the spot, watching her slip into the night. My cock twitched painfully. Luckily, a wind whipped frozen flurries against my flushed face, cooling my passions.

Finally, Brielle faded into the distance. Despite the gloomy situation, hope blossomed. Two weeks ago, she would've let me ravish her against the cold stone building in the alley beyond. Instead, she strode with such a purpose to honor my vow to Ingrid. Though I longed to rush after her and finish what we started, a pang warmed in my being, akin to whiskey on a chilly day. Perhaps she cared for me more than she admitted.

CHAPTER II

BRIELLE

HEAT BILLOWED FROM THE hearth tucked into the corner of the cramped rear room in the herbalist shop. A trail of sweat slid down my spine, causing my perspiration-laden clothes to cling to my damp skin. A thick metallic scent wafted through the air, nearly gagging me. Sadly, the small rectangular window near the top of the wall behind me hadn't provided enough ventilation as I'd engraved the Aralian symbols onto Arianna's new ring. Finally finished, I lowered the etching tool onto the wooden table. It seared against the oak, but I didn't care. My body groaned with fatigue from the hours hunched over the band.

With the etchings completed, the onyx stone glimmered in the candlelight, as if it knew its dark depths would soon serve as Arianna's conduit. I blew out an exhausted sigh, ready to collapse onto the stool beside me. The cuckoo-clock attached to the whitewashed wall in front of me chirped its chipper tune. To my dismay, the timepiece read noon. My nose scrunched at the lateness. I'd hoped to complete this work an hour ago, yet the intricate detailing on the thin band had been more tedious than I'd remembered. However, if I made haste, I could pour cold water over myself and change into clean clothes before Lady Belmont arrived.

In a hurry, I flung the door open. Cool air washed over my skin as I stepped into the herbalist shop. Though the open space was balmy, the temperature felt mild compared to the blazing inferno in the back room. My tense muscles loosened. Potted plants hung from the rafters and lined the windowsills. The shop had the ability to feel like nature had come within, even as frost crawled along the large windows. The welcomed herbal aroma overpowered the tangy metallic scent clinging to my nostrils. I weaved past the labeled cabinets filled with poultices toward the entrance. Sadly, my hope for fresh garments was stripped from me as Arianna peered in through the window, knocking impatiently.

Agitated, I strode to the door and unlatched the lock.

"I should have known you'd arrive at noon on the dot." My fingers rubbed my forehead, trying to untangle the plastered locks from my sticky brow.

Arianna's knuckles blanched as she wrang the handle of a wicker basket. It felt out of place with its delicate weave of soft white reeds, seeming more appropriate for a romantic picnic than this gloomy afternoon.

"If you wanted me to arrive later, you should have said so." The corners of her lips tugged downward, further darkening her somber countenance. Unsurprisingly, she donned mourning black, as if she were a widow already.

I pinched the bridge of my nose, not wanting to argue with the frazzled Lady Belmont. Since hearing of Silas's impending demise, the woman's demeanor had tightened akin to a wind-up toy spun a few notches too many.

She thrust the basket at me. "Sorry. I didn't intend to snap. It's been an excruciating few weeks since my mother's funeral."

My hand laced around the twisted handle. My stomach panged with hunger as the yeasty aroma rose from the receptacle. "I forgive you for your curtness, especially when you come bearing food."

Her tight features smoothed. "This isn't from the grocer? Because I found it on your doorstep. Who would be thoughtful enough to leave you a bushel of baked goods?"

I gulped, assuming who'd delivered this package. A day ago, I'd told Mateo that I wouldn't be able to meet for lunch today. Uncaring as Arianna watched, my fingers shifted the crisp linen covering the treasure trove of treats. My mouth watered over the raspberry preserves, rinds of hard cheese, steaming sourdough, and lemon pastries. Tucked between the sweets was a folded letter. I should have waited until I was alone to read the message, but a sense of delight forced my hand.

Brielle,

I'm certain your cupboards are devoid of provisions, given our last jaunt to the market was days ago. I was concerned that you'd forgo eating again. You may take care of the town, but you also require someone to tend to your needs. Meet me tonight for dinner at the Owl's Nest so that I can make sure you've eaten. I've questioned how you haven't starved to death before our lunches.

-Mateo

"Are you blushing?" Arianna asked, drawing my attention from the note.

A flicker of curiosity pierced through her sober aura. For a heartbeat, her blue irises twinkled with liveliness, and a perk of color tinted her too-pale complexion.

"Of course not." I shoved the message into my pocket and squared my shoulders. "I'm going to change, and then we'll perform the ritual."

The perpetual crease between her brows returned, and whatever ease she'd found once again vanished. She spun the too-large ring on her thumb, and her preoccupied gaze drifted behind me.

"Come on. You can wait in my apartment. I don't want you touching anything, anyway." I walked out of the shop, and she followed.

An icy chill whipped over me, cooling my too hot skin. I rounded the corner, then rushed up the stairs. To my surprise, Arianna pounced up the steps with a catlike agility, keeping pace.

I entered my home, strode through the hallway, and proceeded to the sitting room. Luckily, I'd stowed the empty whiskey bottle and orange peels in the kitchen this morning. Though, my embroidery hoop and vibrant strings lay on the side table next to the floral settee. Red threads weaved about, crossing and entangling in a heaping mess. I plopped the basket beside the jumbled materials. Arianna's soft footsteps padded over the lush rug behind me.

"Have a seat." I pointed to the sofa along the wall.

She didn't sit. Instead, she wandered the living area, taking in every detail of the space. Her hand trailed over the seared marks on the back of the leather chair. Then her focus skimmed over the painting of the full moon festival above the hearth. She approached, studying the floral design on the couch, then shifted to regard the embroidery hoop.

"Your needle work is beautiful." Her fingers traced along the stitched ruby-red poppies. "This must have taken you days."

"It's what I do when I can't sleep. That's the third one I've made this week. My next is an orchid pattern."

Her gentle gaze switched from the needlework to me. "This occupies your nights? That's hard to believe." She assessed me, trying to piece my current life together. Silence stretched over us until she finally perched on the settee. "Go and change. I want to be back by Silas's side before he awakens from his nap."

Without a word, I strode down the hallway and entered my quarters. Instead of dressing, my back pressed against the closed door. Unable to resist, my fingers dug into my pocket and retrieved Mateo's missive. A grin crawled over my face at the sloppy scrawl. My pulse quickened, and a warmth fluttered in my belly. I pressed the note against my chest and shut my eyes, and for the hundredth time, I relived the delicious kiss from a fortnight ago.

A swell of longing mixed with agitation. One simple kiss had muddled my mind and caused this sense of emotional longing to spark within me. Months ago, I would have happily cavorted with Rosalind Collins, uncaring of who got hurt. But I'd declined her because I'd grown fond of Mateo's company, and an entanglement with the blonde would have complicated our companionable connection. Then, overwhelmed with the building emotions, I wept on him like a ninny, then begged for a kiss. That simple peck sparked into life a blazing passion, revealing that I wanted him more than physically.

To my surprise, Mateo didn't ask to court me again. Instead, he acted as nonchalant as ever, like nothing of note had occurred. Initially, the gesture had put me at ease, but over the past two weeks, it had maddened me. Had that been why, when he suggested we spend more time together, I had acquiesced without argument? Then he continued these small, kind gestures, like sending me a picnic lunch that warmed my icy heart in a way that was akin to the spring dispelling the long gloomy months of winter. However, I could never love him to the same degree as I loved Wren. But we carried on, trapped somewhere between friends and something more, because I couldn't deny myself the pleasure of his company.

However, Arianna was waiting. Unable to ruminate longer, I rushed to my wardrobe and tucked the note within my undergarment drawer. A smirk tugged on my lips at the old habit. Hadn't I hidden trinkets from Wren this same way? A dried rose she'd stolen from the inner gardens of the temple, a gold ribbon she'd cut from one of her gowns for the full moon festival, and a lock of her black hair. But the Aralians had confiscated those treasures the same day I'd lost her, and those precious items were gone forever.

With the memory of Wren pressing forward, a flood of guilt replaced the rush of joy I'd felt at Mateo's kindness. These thoughts had also plagued my nights, mixing my desire and curiosity over Mateo with the grief of losing my soul mate.

Unable to linger any longer on my recollections, I peeled off the sweat ladened garment. It fell to the floor in a heap. A chill coursed over me as I yanked the clean garments from my wardrobe. Then, wincing, I slipped the copper-colored day dress over my sticky flesh. Without time to comb out the tangled tresses, I unbraided my hair and smoothed my fingers through my locks. Hurriedly, I twisted the unruly mess into a quick chignon.

With my appearance in some sort of rights, I left my quarters and headed for the sitting area. Yet Arianna's odd behavior gave me pause, causing me to linger in the archway. Unaware of my presence, she rummaged through the gift from Mateo, similar to a sleuth scouring for clues. She lifted the crimson preserves, studying the contents. Sunlight streamed through the frost-covered windows, catching on a few silver strands woven through her blond locks, and highlighting the dark half-moons deepened beneath her crystalline eyes. The news of Silas's illness and the Aralians searching for her had obviously pressed against her as heavily as a knoll stone around her neck.

When I'd visited Belmont Manor yesterday to check on Silas, she'd been in a near tizzy, shuffling books about hoping they held the answers to his ailment. Whenever I attempted to catch her attention, she just muttered under her breath about needing to find a cure. It had been Silas who'd arranged the appointment today, after Arianna had spent her days buried beneath tomes, and I'd been far too busy tending to an outbreak of illness to spend hours preparing the conduit.

In this moment, she seemed to have settled slightly, inquisitively rummaging through the goods. It was a welcomed sight, given how forlorn she'd been.

Sensing my stare, she turned to me. Her eyebrows shot to her hairline.

"What are you doing?" I approached and retrieved the jar from her, then placed it on the side table.

"Simply curious why your nights are unoccupied and you've now received this beautiful bushel brimming with your favorite foods." She studied me, truly seeing me for the first time since Silas had awoken. For once, I wasn't the herbalist assisting her sick husband, but a friend with my own concerns.

"I've been preoccupied with tending to the ailed, and with the entire town paired off, I've been devoid of a bedfellow." I crossed my arms over my chest, trying to hide the truth.

She cocked an eyebrow. "Then who wrote that note and sent the gift? Someone went to a lot of trouble to leave this present."

"We don't have time for this. There is work to be done." I gestured toward the door, trying to deflect. Mateo was a complication that had plagued my thoughts, and if she pushed enough, my confusion would tumble from me.

"I think we do." Arianna tugged me toward the settee to settle beside her. "I knew you were no longer entangling with Everette, but assumed you'd had a potential suitor. At least I'd heard whispers from the maids that you had." She sighed. "Not that you told me."

"And when should we have had a chat? While I spent days tending to the ailing with this damned chill spreading like wildfire through the town? Or when you asked me to help your sister, or at your mother's funeral, or when I came to deliver tonics to Silas while you scoured the library, akin to a mad-woman, searching for a cure?"

Silence hung over us, wrought with the exhaustion we'd both carried for weeks. My stomach growled, punctuating the quiet. Uncaring of our standoff, I yanked the sourdough from the lunch Mateo provided and ripped off the edge, then nibbled at the flaky crust.

She squirmed in her seat. "Well, I'm here and ready to listen."

I swallowed a chunk of bread. "You're here for us to forge a new conduit. Not to cluck about emotions." My nose wrinkled in disgust at the thought of delving into my feelings, and Arianna knew nothing of my interactions with Mateo.

"I have little experience with maintaining friendships. I consider you my friend and my confidant. You understand me and what is happening with Silas. But I value you beyond the help you provide." She placed a tentative hand on mine. "I've relied on you for so much recently. Please rely on me for once."

Arianna smiled softly, tugging at my heartstrings with that darn sincerity that could penetrate the stoniest of resolves.

"Please," she whispered. Perhaps she too needed a distraction, and hearing about my complicated connection with Mateo might give her a brief respite from her own issues.

With a heavy sigh, I capitulated to her request. "Fine, then. It all began at the Kesere festival."

Over the next hour, I unraveled the story, from seeing him in the shadows of Kesere to the kiss the night of the funeral and finishing on our fortnight of platonic companionship. She teetered on the edge of her seat, drinking in the narrative. With half the sourdough eaten and my story finished, she leaned forward, slack jawed.

"Sweet mercy. You must fancy him if you've denied Rosalind and have remained chaste yourself. Do you love him?" Arianna asked.

A pang of hope blossomed in my chest. Was it possible for me to form a relationship with someone else, even if the emotions wouldn't match my affections for Wren? Regardless, Mateo deserved more than my complex circumstance that left me stilted.

"No, I can't. My chance for lasting happiness died with Wren." My hands dusted the crumbs off the copper-colored dress.

"I won't lie to you. I feel something for him. But anything beyond a casual entanglement seems like I'm betraying her."

I expected Arianna to argue, but she said, "I understand. If Silas succumbs to his illness, there'll be no other." Her features hardened, and she gulped, pushing down a swell of sorrow.

"Arianna, I—"

"We are addressing your life, not mine, currently. After we imbue the ring, we will discuss options for saving Silas." She scrubbed her brow, rubbing away the forming lines. She inhaled, then blew out a long exhale, centering herself. A moment later, she reconvened. "You need to sort out your sentiments for him, because you can't keep dragging him along. From this gift, he's already quite smitten with you. If you can't return his emotions, then let him go. But if you care for him, then share these worries with him. He lost his betrothed. Maybe he will understand. Either way, I cast no judgment on you."

My fingers rubbed at my temples, where a headache started to bloom. She was right. If I couldn't reciprocate his affections, I shouldn't continue on. But a slight fraction of my restarted heart whispered into my soul, *what if you could fall in love again?*

CHAPTER 12

BRIELLE

THE DIGNITARIES' MOANS MELDED with the thumping of the drums echoing through the Aralian temple. They writhed with the disciples in training, chasing ecstasy and freeing themselves from their proclivities. The rapturous screams churned in my blood and pooled in my belly, heating my loins. The sweet scent of debauchery and wine filled the space. Like a lioness on the prowl, I searched for my prey. A buxom lady stood fiddling with her goblet. This was the first full moon festival for the new secretary to Lord McConnell, and she'd yet to delve into her wicked desires. A flush crawled along her plump cheeks. My hips swayed to the music, causing the gauzy veil to graze over my breasts. Her pupils dilated as they trailed my nearly nude form, barely hidden by the sheer fabric. I licked my lips, delighted that I'd found such a treasure in this sea of bloated buffoons. But it was my obligation to cleanse those within the high council of their wickedness during these celebrations each month. These acts allowed them to rule Hallowhaven unencumbered from their lustful disposi-

tions. The rituals possessed extreme power, rendering the fortunate few who partook of Delphine to seem ageless.

Tonight, I'd secure the secretary, freeing her of her sinful shackles as we delved into passion. The screams of ecstasy heightened, crescendoing with the beat. Yearning sizzled through me. Ravenous, I beelined for the beauty. Her gaze locked with mine, and a flirtatious grin played on her wide mouth. However, my sultry demeanor dropped as my rival, Jasmine, approached the lady. My jaw clamped shut, holding in an expletive, as she tugged the stunning creature to a bed in the center of the grand receiving room. Jasmine, another orphan clamoring to become a disciple, had continuously undermined me since her arrival.

Undeterred, I searched for the chap who'd had me in raptures at the last full moon celebration, only to spot someone else on her knees with her lips wrapped around his thick cock. He leaned against the table that once brimmed with food, his fingernails digging into the white tablecloth. My blood rushed as his face contorted from his climax.

As my sister swallowed his seed, I scanned the scene. The once bountiful buffet, with roasted meats, sweet treats, and copious amounts of wine, had been picked clean. A councilman mounted a disciple bent over the table, thrusting as her keening crested through the air. I squirmed, pressing my legs together, desperate with need. My head swam with lust as disciples pleasured dignitaries behind the gauzy curtains. I could join any of the oversized beds scattered over the marble floors, barely hiding the acts of intimacy. My sights set on an active group, with two well-endowed middle-aged men partaking of a curvaceous lady.

Tap...tap...tap

Every moan died in the revelers' throats. The music screeched to a halt. My heated body ran cold. Silence stretched through the space, for Delphine was the key to the goddess and her goodness. My knees touched the hard marble floor, and my head dipped into a reverent bow.

My throat dried. Would I receive lashes for not performing these righteous rituals? Would my inability to secure a partner be a stain on my record toward becoming a disciple?

"Sisters and dignitaries, we have a most honored guest who'll be living with us," Delphine's commanding voice boomed. "Wren Delarosa."

My gaze lifted, and my heart thundered. The sepia-skinned beauty lowered herself onto a gilded throne beside Delphine's. Ebony curls haloed her head, and violet eyes pierced against the porcelain mask. My fingers itched to remove the contraption to peer upon her face. The violent fury in her stare was in stark contrast to the pristine painted smile. My attention trailed down her figure, taking in the gold dress she wore. She seemed like a goddess instead of a mere mortal. The shining material plunged, revealing shapely breasts, then pooled over her round hips before flowing down to her feet. A desperate urgency to crawl on my hands and knees to worship her flooded my blood.

"Recommence the festivities!" Delphine slammed her rod over the stone. She tapped her steel-covered fingernails against the gilded armrest.

I blinked, failing to escape the compulsion Wren had pulled me under.

Brielle...

I gasped, disconnecting from the dream so harshly that I nearly toppled from the settee. A moan escaped me, and a throbbing sensation pulsed through my temples. My fingers clutched at my pounding skull as I scanned the dark space, searching for her. Reality slammed into me. Wren would never return, and I was in Presspin.

A shiver snaked down my spine. Goose bumps rose on my flesh. Moonlight streamed through the windows, washing a faint light over the parlor. I squinted at the clock over the mantel, but the once blazing hearth had died.

Knock.

My disoriented focus darted to the hallway leading to my home's entrance. Shadows clung down the corridor. What time was it? After Arianna departed, fatigue had seized me. I'd slunk into the crook of the floral sofa, totally exhausted. Apparently, I'd slipped into a deep slumber, sleeping through the afternoon.

Knock, knock.

"I'm coming," I shouted through my too-dry mouth, certain whoever was here wouldn't relent. My legs wobbled. Stubbornly, my feet stumbled forward. Hopefully, it wasn't a townsperson needing urgent help. With each creeping step, my headache bloomed. It pierced through my eye like a rapier being shoved through it and radiating through my cranium.

Sweat trailed over my skin as I neared the door. Unsteadily, I yanked it open. Without focusing on the dweller, I hissed, "What is it?"

A gust of wind blew icy snow inside, pelting me. The sudden onslaught pushed me off my feet. I stumbled, but warm arms wrapped me in their embrace, holding me steady.

The familiar scents of sage and mint enveloped me.

"Blasts, Brielle. I was worried when you didn't show up for dinner. I came to check on you. Thank the gods I did. You're burning up." Concern coated Mateo's words.

"I'm fine. It's just a headache." I tried to push away, but the sudden dizziness swelled, akin to being in an unsteady sled, spinning on ice. Reality slanted.

"Blasts it is." He lifted me in one fell swoop and nestled me against his chest. "I knew you were pushing yourself too hard. It's possible you caught this nasty chill spreading through town. Didn't you treat two more families this week after tending to Lord Belmont and delivering Mrs. Meriweather's daughter too?"

The door clicked closed. I should have fought him, told him to leave, but pain seized me. Exhausted, I formed a half retort. "I delivered little Cynthia Meriweather last week."

He tutted his tongue and strode down the hallway. "This week, last week, doesn't matter. You're going to run yourself ragged. Which way to your quarters?"

The thought of curling into my bed seemed far more palatable than having him deposit me on the stiff sofa. "Down this hall, through the sitting room, then to the left."

He pressed through the dark parlor, along the corridor, and into my chambers. Bathed in faint moonlight, he weaved past the scattered clothes on the carpet. I sighed in relief as he lowered me onto the pile of pillows. My body melted into the plush cushions. I blinked, trying to focus on him, but an aura danced about him, making it difficult to see.

He tugged the thick green quilt over me, wrapping me in a cozy cocoon. Under this tender care, ease washed over me, unfurling the coiled tension. He withdrew and assessed me. "Do you have any remedies in your apartment?"

"There's some tea in a copper tin in the cabinet next to the woodstove." I nestled deeper into the blanket, trying to find a comfortable position. "But the fire is dead. I'll prepare a brew tomorrow."

He huffed an exasperated sigh, but his tone came out like he was talking to a child. "Do you not remember my letter? You, too, need someone to ensure you are taken care of. I'm going to restart your stove and get your tea ready."

He exited, leaving me with nothing but the intense agony for company. I shut my eyes, fighting the pulsing sensation like my heartbeat panged in my skull. Fatigued, my mind drifted to sleep, and with Wren at the forefront of my thoughts, I returned to her.

"I brought you a sleeping potion." I stepped into the oversized suite. It was far grander than anything I'd ever witnessed. Floor-to-ceiling windows overlooked the private gardens I'd longed to stroll within, the hidden spot as if the Great Beyond were upon earth. The plush rugs softened my footsteps as I approached the window. Green grasses rolled through the lush park, apple trees brimming with fruit encircled the garden, and golden flowers bloomed.

"What are you doing here?" a female voice snapped.

I spun, and the elixir tumbled from my fingers. My shoulders tensed. To my relief, the vial landed on a purple padded rug. My attention didn't lower to the carpet. Instead, it remained transfixed on the most beautiful person. Arched eyebrows highlighted her violet eyes. A beauty mark lay to the right of her regal nose, and her luscious mouth pouted at me. Her chin settled into a point that matched her haughty demeanor.

I knelt and grabbed the elixir, then advanced, drawn to her. She stood before me, captivated. It felt like we were staring into a mirror, viewing an opposite but equal side of ourselves.

"Who are you?" Her words were a whisper, far calmer than her earlier question.

"Brielle Fairchild." My pulsed raced, and her gaze drew me in deeper, akin to falling through the cosmos, untethered to reality.

She tilted her head, drinking me in. "You were at the last full moon celebration."

Wonder softened her features, like I was the most magnificent creature. While a passion stirred within me, heating an overwhelming need to taste of her skin.

Seconds slid past, and frustration replaced her awe. "Why did you let that disgusting Lord Wobbleton have you?"

"It's my duty to perform these acts. How could the high council rule over the territories if plagued by vices?" I stepped back, convinced she wouldn't understand. The common folk were unaware of the truths inside our sacred walls. We acted as the first line of defense against wickedness, and allowing them to partake of our flesh freed them from their lusty nature.

Her hands balled into fists, and without this spelled suite, I'd expected her blight to come seeping out of her akin to poison.

Frustration pinched my brow. "I shall serve the goddess however Delphine sees fit. Though Wobbleton is a grotesque man, our brief entanglement with him brings me one step closer to my dream of *being a bona fide disciple. You're not from our world. You couldn't understand."*

She gritted her teeth, and a deep spark of strength blazed through every fiber of her being. "I've never experienced such unrestrained fury aimed at another human in my life. If I weren't bound to this damn suite and my mask, my power would have sizzled the council member to his bones for touching you."

Shocked, I withdrew, creating distance. Run, my mind screamed, but the idea of being separated from her caused a gaping pit to burrow into my soul.

She stepped closer, leaving a hairsbreadth between us. Confusion laced her tone. "I've never felt such a powerful urge to protect some-one before. Are you a witch sent to tame me? Is that why I dream of you? Because you've cast a spell on me."

"I'm no sorceress." I shook my head.

"I doubt that, enchantress." She leaned forward, locking me into a gentle kiss.

"Brielle."

I blinked, taking in Mateo's tender regard. My pulse skittered. A blush crawled over me, because I had been dreaming about my first physical intimacy with Wren while under his care.

Tentatively, he placed a hand on my forehead. "You're flushed."

His fingers slipped from my brow, then snaked around my waist. With gentle ease, he shifted me to sitting and tucked the pillow behind me.

He turned to the nightstand and picked up an earthen mug set beside a flickering candle that pulsed like a heartbeat. He slid the cup into my grasp. "Drink every drop."

Heat billowed into my palms. I placed the rim against my lips and sipped the bitter, steaming brew. I winced at the taste, mentally noting to buy a jar of honey to mix into it to lighten the flavor. He sat on the edge of the mattress, ready to assist me at the slightest command.

I studied him, notating the contrast between him and Wren. Where she'd been fiery, he acted with gentleness. Where she had blazed with righteous indignation, wanting to be freed from her imprisonment with the Aralians, he approached everything with a peaceful nature. They were like night and day, speaking to different portions of my soul. Perhaps, if I'd been raised by a butcher rather than the Aralians, I would have wed a boy similar to Mateo, cheerful and caring, no matter the situation.

I took a second swig under Mateo's supervision. The hot beverage slid down my throat and settled in my stomach, warming me. My tense muscles slacked, providing a modicum of relief. With a fraction of my wits returned, I spoke. "Will you watch me like a hawk all night? I'm fine."

"I must make sure you finish the remedy, then I'll leave." But the good-natured expression he usually wore never appeared. A crease deepened his smooth brow.

"Then maybe I'll drink it slowly so you're forced to remain by my side." Despite my flirtatious lilt, a kernel of truth lay in my statement.

He gestured to the mug. "Take your medicine."

With each sip, the effects of the tea loosened my hold on reality. Minutes later, only some herbs clung to the mug's bottom. My blood buzzed. The once searing pain halted to a slight pressure. I pushed the cup to Mateo.

"All done," I slurred, then flopped into the bedding, with only the cushions containing my now loose limbs.

A quirk of a smirk tipped. "I'll leave you be. Good—"

"Stay." My palm patted the cool place beside me.

His eyebrows rose to his hairline, then lowered. His lips pulled into a tight line. "That's not the best idea."

"I won't ravage you. Please, I don't want to be haunted by shadowy nightmares. But you're like the sun piercing through the clouds." My hand trailed along the empty spot, uncaring of the flowery prose tumbling from my loose lips. "I'll remain tucked in, and you can sit on top of the covers. Cross my heart, I won't try to seduce you." My fingers moved over my chest.

He groaned and removed his boots, then strode to the opposite side of the bed. He crawled in. The mattress dipped with his weight. Had this been any other night, I may have allowed my desire to rid me of these memories.

He reclined against the pine headboard with his hands shoved into his pockets, as if they'd roam my physique if they were free.

"I'll stay until you fall asleep." Tension laced his gruff tone, as he exerted a tremendous level of restraint.

The statement triggered additional memories, like a gem in a cave, twinkling in the darkness. "That's what I used to say. To my beloved, Wren."

I should regret spluttering out these truths, but the elixir untethered my resolve. As Mateo thawed my icy heart, the frozen memories of her reanimated, haunting me. Our history burned in my soul, trying to break free.

Mateo's tone softened. "You've never mentioned her before, but you don't have to tell me about her tonight. We can speak of this when you're well."

With the tonic loosening my fortitude, the secrets bubbled from me. "If I wait, I'll avoid both the recollections of her and you for your kindness. Under the haze of this tea, I'm unburdened by the torment haunting me. Once I'm done with my tale, you'll finally understand why I can't love you."

Surprisingly, his countenance remained neutral, and he did not press. Seconds passed as we teetered between an emotional intimacy and maintaining the status quo. My fingers fiddled with the fringe of my braid. My pulse elevated akin to plunging off a cliff and into an icy lake below me.

My back lounged against the mound of pillows. Unable to look at him, my stare remained straight ahead. With a shaky breath, I began. "It all started the moment I saw her..."

As if the shackles upon her memory had been unbound, I weaved the tale from our initial encounter to my many visits to bring her sleeping aids and her chats about her existence beyond the temple walls. We'd burned with attraction, and shortly after, a trust formed between us. Although, I spared him the details of our carnality. The hours ticked by, and the tongue-loosening effects of the elixir wore off. Yet I continued to speak of her. Mateo didn't flinch over the Aralians' debauchery, nor my involvement in the religion.

My tale slowed as I reached its climax. Sensing my uncertainty about where it all had ended, he laced his fingers with mine, anchoring me. I didn't pull away. Instead, this simple touch strengthened me.

"One morning, I overheard the disciples talking about sacrificing her. I hadn't ascertained their intentions before then, but most despised the cursed. Before Wren, I, too, hadn't viewed the blighted kindly. I'd been so confident in the Aralians' ways, having been raised in the sect to believe blindly. Yet as we fell deeper in love, I'd considered fleeing with her. With her safety on the line, I couldn't wait to formulate the perfect escape. We had to leave immediately." My nostrils burned with the unshed tears and grief I'd held on to since she'd disappeared.

"My teacher, Helga, was a beast. But her skills as an herbalist were well known throughout Hallowhaven, and she'd often sold her remedies in secret. We weren't allowed to have belongings; we believed they kept us from relying on the goddess. Sadly, I now realize it kept us depdent on the discipleship. She'd hidden her coin in a clay pot, labeled for migraine powder. I'd found the treasure trove weeks prior. Stupidly, I returned to her hiding spot that morning and pocketed the gold. Then I concocted a scheme, creating stronger doses of my sleeping remedy for the guards who blocked the enchantment room where her warded mask was stored, and for her suite."

My jaw ticked, and a bitterness laced my tongue. I ached for the tonic that had made these memories feel akin to bubbles as opposed to heavy weights. Sensing my hesitation, he squeezed my hand. The gesture anchored me to the present, reminding me that the past could no longer hurt me.

"Retrospectively, my ability to thwart the guards had been too easy. Her mask and chamber each possessed a single guard, and both had fallen under my potion's effects. But when I entered her quarters..." I swallowed the engulfing terror. "Wren was gone, and Delphine stood in her place. To this day, I'm unsure who reported me. Could it have been one of my sisters? Or Helga, who'd grown suspicious of my behavior? But it didn't matter. I was as good as dead."

A knot formed in my throat, yet my woeful tale needed to be told. "I attempted to run, but guards waited for me outside the door. Delphine dragged me by my hair down the hall. I can still hear the bells chiming, awakening the temple to come bear witness to my punishment. Those I'd considered my sisters watched as she beat me. At some point, I passed out. Then they dumped me in an alley to die."

Hot tears prickled, but the tidal wave of emotions rolled through me.

"A honeyed voice whispered to me. But my eyes were swollen shut, and I was unable to make out the hooded figure. Streaks of dawn crested over him. I'd assumed he was a reaper sent to claim my soul."

I gulped, trying to remain composed.

"I awoke in a home, with a woman, Martha, tending to me. He'd brought me to his home in Daviel. To my surprise, Martha had been a runaway disciple. This mysterious man rescued many from death after we were deposited in the gutters. As my body grew stronger, she shared with me her experience in the temple and of the territories who suffered under the high council's reign. Eventually, she told me the ugly truth—that everything had been a lie. Aralia wasn't the goddess of light, but the goddess of darkness." I mentally sorted through the information that would stay unspoken. Despite trusting Mateo with my secrets, I didn't share more than he needed to know and kept Martha's lessons about crafting rings for the cursed to myself.

"Once I'd healed, Martha offered me a place in her brothel. But I'd spent years being unable to truly choose my partners. After declining her proposal, the hooded man returned and suggested I move to Presspin, far from the Aralians' reach. I thanked him for his kindness and asked if I could repay him. Oddly, he said that heading to Presspin would be payment enough." I shrugged.

"A few days later, with a few coins in my pocket, I headed north with a couple, the Johnsons, who'd come to Daviel to purchase a dozen lambs."

With my account over, I turned to Mateo, expecting judgment. Instead, sympathy lived in his softened face. To my relief, the last flickers from the candle on the table extinguished, pitching us into darkness. In the comfort of the shadows, I could breathe easier.

"So you see. I can't love you, Mateo. Everyone I've ever cared for has died. My mother, my father, Wren. Even Silas is slipping away. I can't..." A sob caught my throat. "I can't love someone and lose them again."

The emotions I'd kept at bay for years crashed through me. Without my permission, tears spilled from me, leaving a sticky trail down my face. Mateo pulled me into his embrace. His cheek pressed against the top of my head as I wept against him. I should be embarrassed, but perhaps he'd see the truth and relent from his foolish pursuit of me.

His fingers stroked over my back, soothing me. "You are braver than I could have ever imagined. Despite being raised under the lies of the Aralians, you escaped and tried to save your beloved, even though it meant certain death. Wren would be proud of the person you became. You got away from the Aralians and changed. In the years since, you've built a life, cared for an entire town, and made friends. Tonight, you were courageous enough to speak of your experience. I'm beyond honored that you shared this piece of yourself with me, but your original goal of dissuading me from caring for you failed. Your story has showed me that you, Brielle, are worth the wait."

CHAPTER 13

BRIELLE

SUNLIGHT STREAMED THROUGH THE gossamer curtains, bathing me in the soft winter glow. I stretched, akin to a cat soaking up the sunshine. The migraine elixir and a good night's sleep had relaxed my muscles. I curled deeper into my bedding. The soothing scent of mint and sage lingering on my sheets caused an ease to spread through me. A clink of someone rummaging through the kitchen just beyond drew my attention out of this blissful haze.

Jolted to reality, I scrambled to sitting and peered toward the doorway. Mateo had stayed the night after I'd jabbered about my feelings, then bawled into his chest like an idiot. My hand scrubbed over my face. Mateo had yet again crumbled another portion of my walls. Despite only sleeping, our relationship had transformed into something deeper. I sucked my teeth. My mind whirled, trying to assess what this meant.

Before I could put myself to rights, the clinking of boots echoed down the hallway, breaking through my ruminations.

Self-conscious, my fingers pinched my cheeks to brighten my gaunt coloring, then unraveled my braid and smoothed my hair. My auburn locks cascaded around me. My palms ran over the crumpled blouse I'd fallen asleep in. My heart pounded with an unexplainable anticipation as his footsteps reached the entrance.

"You're awake." A whisper of a grin pulled on his lips. In one hand, he held a plate brimming with eggs, bacon, and toast, and in the other, a steaming earthen mug.

My mouth watered, not only over the food, but over him. His chestnut locks were slicked back, and his hazel eyes sparkled as he took me in. A tunic clung to his lean frame and was left open at the collar, displaying a hint of his hard pectoral muscles. My hands itched to touch him, but the sensation burned deeper than a fleeting lust.

He strode forward and settled the meal on the nightstand beside me. I cocked an eyebrow, curious about where he'd found the supplies because my cupboards had been bare since yesterday.

He rubbed his nape. Then, sensing my questions, he said, "I awoke at dawn." He shrugged. "You were still sleeping when I snuck away to my house. I bathed and changed, then headed to the grocer and bakery. Your cabinets are brimming with enough food to sustain you for a fortnight at least."

I stared at him, slack jawed. Then registered that his return home, subsequent errands, and cooking breakfast meant I'd slept the morning away. In a panic, I pushed the blankets off and shifted to crawl out of bed.

His brow furrowed, and he pressed his heavy hands to my shoulders, anchoring me to the spot. "You are not getting up until you finish your meal. There is a notice on the storefront window stating that the shop will remain closed until noon. If an emergency occurs, they can come upstairs, and I'll decide if it's urgent enough to rouse you."

"Noon." My nose wrinkled.

"You're lucky I didn't place a notice saying *closed for the day*." He crossed his arms over his chest.

I snorted at the stoic expression. "Perhaps you have a bit of brooding in you after all."

My stomach grumbled. With a groan, I capitulated to his will. My back leaned against the headboard, then my hand reached for the cup.

I took a long sip, savoring the coffee's dark flavors and the heavy splash of cream with a dollop of honey. A genuine smile stretched across my face at this simple, domesticated scene. Though I should send him home, my stony resolve had been weakened by his compassion.

There had been a shift in our relationship, but not the one I'd suspected. Instead of judging me for my past transgression, he treated me with the same tender care he always had. His features didn't fill with pity when he looked at me now, nor did a stiffness enter his mannerisms.

He nestled onto the foot of the mattress, keeping his distance. But as our gazes locked, my heart melted. My gods, he was beautiful inside and out. Yet my mind still reeled. Why did he remain by my side after everything I'd told him? Did he truly care about me this deeply? An unspoken intimacy bubbled, this unaccustomed mix of sexual tension and emotional yearning.

Unable to withstand this pressure building between us, I jested. "I'm sure you are going to watch me like a hawk until I finish my entire breakfast, right?"

"Of course, after last night, I've decided that you are helpless without me." A flicker of a smirk tugged. "Now eat up."

We settled into a companionable silence. I grabbed the bacon from the plate and munched on it, nibbling each piece slowly. As I reached the last bite, a lustful longing filled Mateo's stare. Seductively, I sucked my fingers, dragging out the sensual act. A flush of color washed over him. He licked his lips like I was the savory treat. Our mutual attraction had always smoldered, but since last night the desire sizzled. His muscles tightened, ready to pounce.

To my disappointment, he shook his head, freeing himself from his primal compulsion. A seriousness entered his expression. A pang burrowed into my belly. Though I'd cracked my heart open similar to a shell holding an egg, I wasn't quite certain what lay within.

"Brielle, I—"

Knock, knock, knock.

Relief washed over me as his attention switched from me to the door. His shoulders slumped. I shifted to rise, but he shook his head, then exited.

With him gone, I noticed Mateo had been busy with other household chores as I slumbered. He'd collected the scattered clothing and placed them in the basket for the laundress near the door. Even the cup from the night before and my customary half-empty whiskey bottle had been removed.

I considered following after him but wasn't prepared to delve into what my revelations meant for us. Instead of fretting, I plopped a heaping spoonful of eggs onto the bread and ate. The savory flavor danced in my mouth. It would be truly delightful to wake up to a meal like this every morning. My jaw froze mid chew as my mind focused on our undefined relationship. Would Mateo revisit his original request to court me, having been undeterred from my tale? Uncertainty tightened in my chest. If he asked me now, I'd have a much harder time denying his proposition after sharing my story. Despite my insistence that I couldn't love him, I was unable to shake the warmth coursing through my veins, reviving me from this stasis. I wasn't a dunce—he was the reason for this change within me.

A few minutes later, he came sauntering through the door, clutching a missive with a familiar seal.

I shoved the final bit of toast into my mouth, wiped my palms on my dingy blouse, and took the letter from his outstretched hand. The Belmont crest, with its lone prominent pine tree in front of a mountain scene, gleamed.

Concerned, my thumb slipped under the crimson wax and plucked it open. My ease diminished bit by bit with each line of the hasty scrawl. I sighed, certain that whatever Mateo had wanted to say would have to wait. My fingers folded the letter and tucked it into my pocket.

"What is it? Is everything all right?" Concern filled Mateo's gaze.

I picked up the mug and downed the room-temperature coffee. "Silas woke up with a fever. I must go, but…" I pursed my lips, uncertain about how to phrase these complicated emotions swirling within me. "I need some time to think. Last night…I've never told anyone the full breadth of what happened to Wren. And my feelings for you…"

"Your feelings for me?" His eyes shone with hope.

"I don't know what they are or what they mean. I'm confused. Please give me a few days to be alone with my thoughts."

His face fell. Without thinking, I lowered the cup to the nightstand and rose. He remained frozen as my body inched closer. I approached and wrapped my arms around him. His tense chest released a sigh. I tilted my gaze to him and allowed myself the luxury of drinking him in. He was so beautiful. I couldn't help myself as my lips pressed against his. Unlike before, where our mouths melded in passion, I tried to convey the complications. That despite my bravado, he meant more to me than a heated entanglement.

His fingers snaked into my hair, and my palms trailed over his back, wishing I could seal us in this moment. He was tenderness, care, and everything I swore I would never want, but hadn't realized I needed. Overwhelmed by these percolating emotions melding with my grief, I pulled away.

"Thank you, Mateo."

"I'm here when you're ready, Brielle. I wasn't lying when I said you are worth the wait."

CHAPTER 14

BRIELLE

THE SOUR SCENT OF sickly sweat lingered in the master suites of Belmont Manor, like this illness lay within the gilded papered walls. Though I'd grown accustomed to the pungent aroma that accompanied blazing temperatures, I hadn't expected Silas to suffer from the sudden onslaught so soon. The brooding lord reclined wearily against the sleigh headboard, scowling at me as if his will alone could heal him. Yet his clipped breaths punctuated the air, melding with the sound of my boots padding over the soft rug. His tunic clung to his withering form, damp from perspiration. A knot twisted in my gut as I approached. I lowered the leather satchel brimming with tonics I'd brought to the nightstand and studied him. His complexion had blanched since my last visit days ago. Dark bags deepened under his eyes, and his cheeks had hollowed.

Undeterred, I began my silent assessment by taking his pulse, noting the rapid rhythm. Then my fingers snaked along his forehead, which blazed akin to an inferno. He glowered at me like I was his childhood nursemaid keeping him from an outing.

He swatted my hand away. "Stop fussing over me."

My jaw ticked. As his ailment progressed, he would become difficult to handle, similar to most men.

"My apologies, *my lord*." Sarcasm coated my tone. "Pardon me for rushing over here to tend to you instead of lounging in bed devouring..." My mouth clamped shut, withholding Mateo's name, and hissed, "Breakfast."

"Breakfast." Silas rolled through the word with a hint of disbelief.

Ignoring him, my focus shifted to my medical bag, and I rummaged through the elixirs, searching for the willow bark powder to lower his temperature.

"From Grey's report, a man answered your door. I'm assuming it wasn't a meal you were consuming, but the young Mateo Re—" A cough rattled through him, breaking his haughty demeanor.

My gaze shifted from the satchel to him. When he pulled his fingers from his mouth, blood coated them. That gnawing pit churned within me. His ailment escalated with each passing day. I withdrew a clean handkerchief from my bag and handed it to him.

To my dismay, his condition didn't align with the chill afflicting the town. A low fever, headache, and nasal congestion affected them. Whereas Silas's symptoms mirrored those of the progressing wasting illness. That sliver of hope vanished. In my training with Helga, I'd had a few instances of tending to the cursed as they suffered from the sickness. The paltry remedies they provided to the blighted were not to keep them comfortable as the ailment ate away at them, but so they could drain every drop of power coursing through their bodies.

"I've always known you to flaunt your conquests, but you mention nothing of this chap? I might be stuck in this damned manor, but the maids whisper, and my wife confides in me," he wheezed, breaking my ruminations.

"Perhaps we should focus on your ailments instead of my love life." My fingers pulled out a thick elderberry elixir for his respiratory afflictions from the leather bag.

"*Love?*" He cocked an eyebrow.

His curious stare blazed into the side of my face. Unwilling to delve into Mateo and what these complex feelings were, I changed the subject. "Where is that chatty wife of yours anyway?"

Unable to resist the urge to speak of his beloved, he took the bait. "Arianna's probably in the library, with her nose in a medical tome. She's already read through an entire bookcase of them. She's determined to find an answer and..."

As he droned on about Arianna, I poured the sticky black syrup into the cup, then mixed in another vial of blended herbs to keep his airways clear. Then I plucked a final mix of willow bark powder to counteract the fever. His voice melded with the clinking of the spoon against the tumbler as my brain whirled around the word *love*. Why did my pulse surge at the mere thought of loving Mateo? I couldn't deny these percolating feelings that rose akin to champagne bubbles filling my belly whenever he spilled into my mind.

"I'm worried about Arian—"

"I don't know how I feel about him." I spun and handed Silas the medicine as we spoke in unison.

"What are you speaking of?" His fingers wrapped around the etched glass discolored by the sticky elixir, and he downed it in one gulp. He grimaced at the unpalatable taste.

"Mateo. What were you talking about?"

"Arianna, of course, and her endless need to find a cure for me." He lowered the cup to the nightstand with a clink. Fatigue coated his expression from a mix of physical and mental exhaustion.

My focus shifted from Mateo and to the present. My jaw ticked as the potential solution crested my mind. "Let me write Martha, and we can lay this to rest."

His features hardened to that of granite. His nostrils flared, and an imperiousness entered his tone, as if he were speaking to a subject and not a friend. "No. This is my final decision. I've never used my authority as the overseer of Presspin against you, but I swear to the gods if you write her, I'll have the constable throw you into the brig with instructions to only let you out after I die. Shall you spend the winter imprisoned? Or with your whatever the blasts Mateo is to you?"

"You wouldn't." My palms pressed into my hips, but an unfamiliar menacing gleam burned in his golden gaze.

"Friend or not, I killed a dozen Aralians and left a radius of ash a mile wide in my wake to protect Arianna. Locking you in the brig would be the lesser of my sins to ensure her safety."

My stomach twisted. He wasn't bluffing.

"As you wish, my lord," I hissed through my clenched teeth and bowed like the underling he treated me like in the moment.

Frustrated, I extracted the remaining tonics and placed them on the nightstand for the next few days, as the fever hopefully subsided.

"Take the elixirs four times a day." My body dipped into a low curtsey.

He huffed an exasperated sigh and grabbed my wrist. "Wait."

I yanked myself free, unwilling to be manhandled by him.

"I'm sorry I have to go to these lengths to protect Arianna and Presspin. If the Aralians come, do you believe they won't kill you? I'm the overseer until I die, and I will do my best to protect my people, my friends, and my beloved until my final breath. It's why Peter, with my blessing, is reforming the militia, just in case our plan on hiding Arianna is thwarted. But we can't allow even a whisper of her presence to leave our town. Please don't be angry with me for making the hard choices no one wants to make."

I gritted my teeth, but the boiling frustration simmered to a mild agitation. If the Aralians found me alive, they'd execute me and imprison Arianna until they drained her dry. A shudder crossed over me and the royal purple suite crested into my memory. Would Arianna disappear in a similar fashion to Wren, never to be seen again?

"Fine. I won't write to her for now." My fingers laced around the soft leather handle, and I tugged my bag over my shoulder. "Get some rest. I'll check on you in a few days."

He gave a curt nod, and I hurried away. As I exited the suite, a frazzled Mrs. Potter slammed into me, dashing my plans for escape. I clenched my jaw, not in the mood for the maid's sharp tongue.

Her brown eyes widened like saucers as she took in my face. Then, to my shock, relief washed over her expression. "Thank the gods you're still here. Hurry, it's my lady and her sister. They're having a row. Come quickly. You seem to be the only person capable of talking sense into that stubborn chit." She tugged my arm and yanked me down the hall.

Thrown from one Belmont emergency and into another. I shook off Mrs. Potter's grasp, but I followed her hurried footsteps. We pressed through the passageway and turned toward the servant staircase. The older woman huffed as she sprinted down the steps with me in tow. Finally, we veered left and headed down an unfamiliar hallway.

Muffled shouts echoed through the narrow corridor, coming from a room at the end of the hall. The sisters were amid a heated discussion.

"That way to the conservatory." A huffing Mrs. Potter pointed ahead, then stopped. She stooped over, drawing shallow breaths.

The clattering of broken ceramic crashing against tiles replaced the shouts. I quickened my pace, rushing past Mrs. Potter. Seconds later, I arrived at the spot where the commotion originated. With a steadying breath, I pushed the oversized mahogany door. It creaked open, but the pair didn't acknowledge my presence as my boots clicked across the threshold and into the airy hothouse. The sisters' bickering bounced from the floral tiled floors and drifted to the high vaulted glass ceilings. A storm had rolled in, casting the naturally lit area in deep shadows. Disarray denoted this once beautiful oasis.

"Goddess above! What makes you think I'd want to celebrate my birthday with random strangers? I hate this damned place," Naomi shouted, drawing my attention to the pair. She pointed a finger at Arianna. A crimson stain flushed her full cheeks, and fury contorted her face. Surprisingly, the girl no longer touted the ratty robe and slippers from before. Instead, she donned a black mourning dress of the finest silk. Her dark appearance oddly matched the decaying plants scattered throughout the abandoned conservatory.

Arianna stood frozen a few paces from me and opened her mouth to interject. Simultaneously, Naomi picked up an empty earthen pot off a worn metal table with peeling lacquer. She chucked it at her sister, who dodged it with ease. The rust-red planter smacked against the brick wall, causing shards to scatter over the dusty tile floor.

My gaze flicked to the elder of the two. Arianna's shoulders rose and fell. Her lips remained straight-lined. An internal battle waged behind her tightly drawn features, like she would snap at any moment. To my horror, wisps of smoke curled from her balled fists. My mind reeled. Her power shouldn't be this unbridled with the newly forged ring. Something was wrong.

But before I could step between the sisters and deescalate the situation, Naomi strode toward Arianna, her hands flailing wildly about her, akin to a madwoman. "I want to go home. That's what I desire for my birthday. But I can't, can I?"

I leapt between the women, blocking Naomi's progress.

"Arianna, leave." I held Naomi's withering stare. The door creaked open, then closed, leaving us alone.

"How dare you interfere with—"

Smack.

Naomi clutched her cheek. Rage boiled in her tense expression, but she remained silent.

"You spoiled little brat. You're arguing with your sister because she wants to host a birthday celebration for you all while she's dealing with everything else? Or are you so dense that you haven't noticed? Didn't you tell Nellie you wanted to be a physician? Yet you've overlooked the obvious symptoms of the terminally ill man upstairs?" My lip curled.

Her face fell, and the coiled anger cooled in her eyes. However, she didn't drop her feral snarl. "What do you mean?"

My fingers pinched the bridge of my nose. "Silas is dying, Naomi. He won't make it to spring. Yes, you lost your mother, but that doesn't give you the right to cause everyone such gods' damncd misery."

I brushed past her, not waiting for her to speak. I scoured the cobweb-filled space, found a broom nestled in the corner, and grabbed it. As I spun, I nearly whacked Naomi, who'd followed on my heels.

"Here, go clean something." I pressed the broom into her grasp.

Her nostrils flared, but she didn't argue. Instead, she began sweeping. My jaw clenched at the scene, but Mateo's words from the night prior crested forward. I'd dealt with the loss of my loved ones by forming a new life. Naomi had spent weeks sulking in her quarters. She needed a fresh start. My teeth gnawed on the inside of my lip. To the best of my knowledge, she hadn't returned to the Artist Alcove. No, she needed an occupation to busy herself with.

I scanned the dilapidated conservatory. Soft flurries drifted over the floor-to-ceiling window, encapsulating the area. Brick lined the back wall, and glass surrounded the rest of the room, like we were in a snow globe. Nestled amongst the red stone lay a massive wood stove, which had likely blazed all winter long to overcome the icy temperatures. Broken planters filled with dried dirt that had likely housed fruit trees created a path leading to a rickety cast-iron bench. Near the hearth sat a table with peeling lacquer covered in dusty clay pots and vials. Whoever this place once belonged to had some herbalist skills, if the old mortar and pestle covered in cobwebs were any indication. An idea formed in my mind. One that would keep the girl occupied and pull her from this depressive episode while also helping me. Though I hated to admit it, Mateo was right. I had been running myself ragged.

"I have a proposition." My back pressed against the wall and layers of grit likely seeped into my white blouse.

"I'm not interested in becoming your bedfellow." Her gaze remained on the spot she cleaned, pretending the broken shards of clay were far more interesting than anything I had to say.

A barking laugh emitted from me. "What would I do with a sullen *child* like you?"

"I'm only a few years younger than Mateo, and I'm sure you'd happily drag him into your bed." She pushed the fractured pieces into a pile. They scraped along the tile, punctuating the beat of silence between us.

"Regardless, he's more mature than you. But we aren't talking about him. We are speaking of you. Come and work with me as my apprentice. The town has kept me busier than I care to admit, and with Silas's illness progressing, I'll need someone else with a knowledge of herbal remedies and medical practices to assist me."

She stopped and spun toward me. She jutted her chin. "And what would I get?"

"I'd pay you, obviously, and provide you with plants to help revive this conservatory. You can't return to Krella, but we can bring home to you. I'll talk with some farmers who have greenhouses and see if they're willing to spare some saplings. Perhaps you'd considered asking your sister to spend the funds she'd have used on a silly party to restore this space. Also, you'd be free from Belmont Manor at least a few hours every day."

She worked her jaw, but she didn't fight me. Instead, she leaned the broom against the old table and strode forward with her palm extended. "Fine. I'll become your apprentice. It's better than staying here."

We shook hands. Hopefully this agreement would be mutually beneficial instead of leading to more problems.

CHAPTER 15

BRIELLE

PURPLES AND PINKS TRAILED through the sky, casting a beautiful cascade of colors over the snow-covered mountain. A shade of violet blended into the sunset, reminding me of the gorgeous hue of Wren's eyes. The sweet, sharp pine scent wafted through the air, tickling my nostrils. However, the once heavy feelings tied to her disappearance didn't weigh on my shoulders like a knoll stone. Perhaps spending two weeks weeping in my room over her absence had finally freed me. Today I'd crested through this odd sensation where I could remember her without being drowned in grief. Her death still hurt, but with each passing day, I could view the memories and relive fragments of joy along with the sorrow.

Feeling lighter, I hastened down the sidewalk to the shop. The purple tint washed over my storefront, as if Wren were here, and in remembering her, I'd received her blessing to live. In a few quick strides, I closed the distance to the entrance and stepped in. The bell rang overhead, announcing me. Seconds later, the rear door opened, and Naomi peeked her head through the crack. Her tight features slacked, and she walked out.

"Where've you been all day?" She crossed her arms over her chest, glaring at me like she was my supervisor instead of my subordinate.

"I delivered tonics for the Monroes and the Gundersons, then checked on Mrs. Johnson, who's having another flare-up in her joints." I approached the counter and placed my now empty medical satchel on it. "What did you do all day? Still tinkering with that new blend for respiratory ailments?"

She ran her fingers over her stained apron, splattered with a colorful speckling of herbal powders. "It's stronger, just not quite right yet. Once it's ready, I can help so many people. Maybe Tabitha's consumption or Silas's sickness." Her brows knitted together.

"Speaking of Tabitha and your propensity for concocting remedies. Do you ever plan on telling your sister about your secret life in Krella? If you told her the truth, she'd understand why you've been so damned scornful about coming here." My hands settled on my hips.

Though her sour countenance hadn't fully vanished, she'd shown me hints of the person she'd likely once been. No longer being stuck in Belmont Manor had made her far more palatable. As I grieved Wren, she'd put herself to work, using my medical tomes to create elixirs and minding the storefront. I'd been true to my word and had provided her with saplings from the farmers around town to restore her conservatory. Even Arianna had shifted the funds from a frivolous party toward the project. Though the sisters' relationship was still strained, they'd found a way to coexist. It helped that Arianna spent her time training with Peter, fussing over Silas, and searching the library for answers, while Naomi remained either here or in the hothouse. But many unspoken truths lay between the sisters.

Naomi brushed past me, grabbed a watering can, and headed for the windows. She approached a line of potted herbs perched on the sill, basking in the last traces of the fading sunlight. "I'll tell Arianna about my secrets when you stop avoiding Mateo. He came this afternoon. He asked me not to tell you, but the man is concerned over your well-being, for some reason. Why he fusses over you when you are so damned aloof boggles my mind."

I should ignore the bait. However, I missed him. I'd distanced myself from him over the last fortnight to sort through this intense grief I carried for Wren. Though I still felt the ache of her absence, approaching the feelings head on had helped me cope with the pain I'd been burying. In processing the overwhelming emotions, the guilt I had been holding on to surrounding her death eased until they were akin to a wound being stitched together. Simultaneously, my absence from Mateo caused a new pain to blossom. I longed for his smile, our lunches, his attentive care, and how he made the most mundane parts of my day enjoyable. My heart ached to be close to him, but I worried that these burgeoning feelings weren't enough.

"Was he well?" I followed behind Naomi as she sprinkled water into a sage plant.

She snorted. "Of course not. He's lovesick."

"It's better this way." My gut twisted. I'd been so certain that Mateo deserved so much more than I could give him.

Naomi harrumphed.

I scurried toward a pot with some faded leaves and plucked them off, then tucked them into my pocket. "I've already had and lost my soul mate."

She lowered the watering tin to the sill with a clink. "Shall I smack you out of your foolishness like you slapped me? Why are you and Arianna so obsessed with this idea of mates? As if you have no choice in your destiny. I knew Arianna's head was often filled with romantic dribble, but given your carnal nature, I would have never thought you'd be so close-minded. You'd allow some unknown entity to make a decision for you? It's such ridiculous hogwash. As for me, I control my own fate. This silly notion of soul mates would never sway me. Give yourself permission to love him, Brielle. You're halfway there already. Just take the leap."

CHAPTER 16

MATEO

My HANDS DIPPED INTO the soapy water in the basin. The faint scent of lye and lemon wafted from the suds sticking to my dinner plate. Moonlight filtered through the window, illuminating my kitchen with a soft glow. My fingers scrubbed the etched glass a bit too briskly as I chastised myself for breaching my agreement with Brielle this afternoon. I'd promised her I'd be patient but couldn't help this constant concern eating at me. This morning, I found myself striding straight to her shop, after realizing her cupboards had probably grown bare. Yet when I'd entered, the spirited Naomi sat behind the counter, deflating my original intention of seeking out the likely starving herbalist. After a clipped exchange between myself and the taciturn Ms. Park, I slipped away to find solace somewhere else.

With the tavern brimming with memories of Brielle, I'd spent the past fortnight seeking respite at the boxing club. I'd spent hours under Liam's instruction and conversing with Vincent when he could sneak away from the mounting responsibilities of Belmont Manor. I'd even signed up for the reforming militia with Vincent to further occupy my time. Despite the comradery, an ache still lingered in Brielle's absence.

With my dishes washed, my hand wrapped around a towel from the drawer and began wiping the sparkling silver cutlery. Perhaps I should have left her home after I'd given her the migraine tonic a fortnight ago? Yet having heard her firsthand account over her past, I couldn't help but harbor a deepening ardor for her.

Knock, knock, knock.

My brow furrowed as I lowered the towel and cutlery to the counter. My attention shifted toward the entrance. Leaving the kitchen, my feet padded over the wood floors to the foyer. Perhaps Vincent had stopped by for dinner after all?

As I opened the door, my once steady pulse elevated. Brielle clutched a lantern blazing through the darkness. It cast a soft glow over her auburn tresses and fretful expression. Stars twinkled behind her. I gaped, surprised she'd trekked down the snow-covered path in the middle of the night to see me. Despite the frigid weather, she wore a black woolen cloak over her olive day dress. My mind sputtered, working to piece the scene together. Had she arrived in the shadows like a harbinger of doom, coming to cut off our budding connection?

She cleared her throat, breaking this tense moment buzzing between us. She shifted forward and latched the lantern onto the empty hook along the eaves of the awning. Light cast away the shadows and drew my focus toward her uncharacteristic nervousness. Uncertainty panged within my gut. My arms crossed over my chest, to guard my heart and these burgeoning feelings for her.

"Blasts, this is difficult." Her boots clipped against the hardwood on the porch as she returned to her place before me. Yet her focus remained beyond me on the light. "I should have waited until the morning, but I couldn't wait a moment longer. Like my damned legs had a mind of their own and led me straight here."

My shoulders tensed, but my body remained rooted to the spot. Should I invite her in? But from her shifty motion, she'd likely flee if I spoke first. Seconds dragged. My heart beat with a mix of longing and terror.

Finally finding the resolve, she balled her fists and drew in a sharp breath. I readied myself for her permanent rebuke. Naomi must have told her of my presence at her storefront, leading here her to set me straight. I shouldn't have pushed; I should have waited for her to come to me.

"I've missed you, Mateo."

My brain spun, shocked that her statement wasn't a perpetual goodbye.

She continued, undeterred by my shock. She shrugged, as if this weren't a pivotal conversation unfolding between us. "What can I say? You've charmed me. And this damned insistent need to be close to you won't go away. It just keeps getting worse."

Her features softened, and that beautiful, vulnerable woman in Ingrid's sketch emerged.

"I've decided that you can court me." The phrase whooshed from her.

I stared, slack jawed, certain I'd misheard her. My fingers rubbed my forehead, until her sentiment sunk into my thick skull. To my relief, my time with her had left an impression. Enough that she'd allow me to court her. My heart soared.

"Did you hear me?" She pressed her palms to her hips.

I stepped closer, leaving a handsbreadth between us. Her stern countenance softened. Heat sizzled, despite the chill nipping at the air. A well of emotions lived in her eyes, as if she were allowing me this secret version she hid. The expression disintegrated the worries I'd held that my sentiments were one-sided. Finally free from fear, the swelling emotions I carried burst to the surface. In this moment, I realized I loved her. A deep longing to express my ardor blazed through me, like a fire sparking to life. Without a word, I tugged her into my embrace, relishing in the warmth of her body searing into my chest.

The light hint of whiskey laid on her breath. Desperate to taste her, I dipped my head and placed my lips against hers. The second we kissed, frenzy fueled my blood. She'd awakened a dormant piece of me, a piece I'd feared died with Ingrid. Equally eager, she drew my tongue into her mouth with sensual sucks. Lightning shot down my spine, fueling my desire. I pivoted and pushed her against the doorframe, half mad with lust. Simultaneously, her hands settled on my waist, drawing me near. Need pulsed through me, clouding my mind of anything aside from devouring her. My lips skated to her earlobe, nibbling on the tender flesh. Her breathing escalated, turning into the sweetest pants, punctuating the night air. A breeze blew over us. Goose bumps rose on Brielle's skin, cooling her passions.

"Mateo, we should stop. Your vow."

Withdrawing, I took in her beautiful face, the slope of her perfect nose, the slant of her catlike emerald eyes, and her high cheekbones. I grinned, akin to a pirate who'd captured a siren. I leaned my forehead against hers, breathing in the sweet vanilla and amber aroma that lingered in my dreams.

"This past fortnight has been miserable without you. I'd thought I was living after Ingrid died, but the time I spent with you helped me realized I'd been surviving. You brought me back to life, Brielle. I'd been curious about you because of how Ingrid portrayed you in her last sketch, but as we became better acquainted, I came to understand you. You wear your strength like an armor protecting your gentle heart. You've suffered so much. Let me act as your shield and care for you so you may have a place to be free of the world's burdens. Lay your worries on my shoulders so I can be your respite."

"That sounds terribly tedious." Despite the jesting phrase, it came out in a breathy whisper of awe.

"It's what you do for those you love." My thumb traced her cheek, hoping my sentiment would soak into her skin.

"You love me?" She breathed out the question.

"I do."

Silence washed over us. Worried she might think I'd expect her to reciprocate, I held up my hands, showing my palms. "It's all right if you don't—"

She lunged for me and clamped her lips over mine, sealing my words with a rough kiss. My mind fizzed, akin to the bubbles of sparkling wine floating to the top of a flute. Reality bent as she devoured my mouth.

Panting, she pulled away. Her emerald gaze darkened. She shifted from the doorframe, out of my grasp, and into the foyer. Her fingers untied the knot at her throat and tugged at it. The cloak she wore dropped to the hardwood. Understanding seized me, and with hurried steps, I entered the vestibule and closed the door behind me.

Like a lioness on the prowl, she pounced, reigniting our kiss. The force of her movements caused me to stumble so my back smacked against the wall. The plaster pressed through my cotton tunic. Her lips disconnected from mine, skating over my throat and stopping at my pulse point. Blood rushed toward my eager cock, triggering it to strain against my breeches, pressing against her belly.

Mischief filled her expression as she lowered to her knees.

I gulped as she unbuckled my pants, then slid them and my undergarments down far enough to expose my throbbing dick.

"My gods." Brielle's hot breath trailed over my erect shaft.

I panted, too eager for this sort of game, yet far too invested to halt her. Her lips wrapped around my cock. Heat rushed through me. She licked the head in a swirling motion, causing lightning to shoot down my spine. A groan escaped me. Fueled by my year of celibacy, my hands snaked into her smooth auburn locks. Sensing my desire, she drew me into her mouth. Minutes skittered by as she bobbed on my cock, pulling me deeper into her mouth. Stars splattered behind my eyes as I teetered toward my climax. The building pressure filled like a balloon ready to burst. My grasp on her silken locks tightened, and I fought the overwhelming urge to thrust deeper. If we continued, I'd spill into her throat before we'd even entangled.

"If you don't stop, I'll…"

To my horror, the vixen quickened her pace, pushing me toward the edge of combusting. My hardened member pulsed. Unwilling to be handled by her, I yanked her away.

She smirked, delighted by the roughness.

"I have plans for you, and I wasn't joking about keeping you trapped in my bed for days once I allowed myself to have you." I released my hold on her and pulled up my pants, sheathing my painfully engorged dick. Brielle had experienced many paramours, while I'd only had one before now. But my lack of experience wouldn't be my undoing. No, she'd find her pleasure first.

"Stand up." I offered her my hands, pulling her to her feet. Curiosity colored her expression. In one fell swoop, I reversed our roles, pushing her against the wall in my stead. Hungrily, I dropped to my knees, prepared to worship her. My fingers skated up her ankles, caressed her calf, to her thigh, then settled upon her undergarments. I peeled off the damp fabric, inch by inch, until it fell to the floor. Finally freed, I shimmied under her skirt, inhaling the heady scent of her arousal. My palms trailed her leg, then placed her left knee over my shoulder, opening her to me.

My hands pressed into her ass. Her breathing escalated as my face hovered near her damp curls. My tongue delved into her slick folds, flicking the pearl at its apex. A sharp inhale escaped her, and her hands clawed at my shoulders, trying to find purchase. Undeterred, my lips plucked upon the tender bud, causing Brielle to melt. In this blissful haze, I continued my ministrations, devouring her intimate flesh until her keens filled the silent night.

Minutes ticked past like mere seconds. My arousal heightened with each delicious moan, drawing out her pleasure until she whimpered for release.

"Please," she whined.

She trembled, swaying off balance. Unwilling to relent, I dug my fingers into her fleshy rear, steadying her. As she melted, I sucked at the sensitive nub until her knees wobbled. Her panting sighs elevated. Fueled by her desperation, my lips latched against the bundle of nerves. Her body quivered, pulsing with the ecstasy. A scream ripped through her.

I trailed gentle kisses along her thigh, to her knee and her ankle, while sliding her from standing to sitting.

As I left the cozy cocoon of her skirts and found her panting against the whitewashed wall, similar to a limp rag doll, a grin of satisfaction crossed over me. Her legs bowed akimbo, and her green dress rode up to her creamy thighs.

"My...gods...I would have let you court me sooner had I known you had such a wicked way with your tongue," she sputtered between ragged breaths.

I barked a laugh, then raked my hand through my mussed hair. A moment of mirth overcame the smoldering lust. Warmth beat within my chest as I drank her in where she was satiated in the foyer's corner.

As the bubbling levity lessened, yearning reentered her eyes. My dick strained against my trousers, aching to fill her. Sensing my need, she stood. Her fingers skimmed along the copper buttons on the front of her wool day dress. With a seductive slowness, she undid the fastenings one by one. The fabric whooshed off her creamy skin and pooled on the floor. With a smirk, she slid off her chemise until she was bare before me. My resolve fizzled as I stared at her full breasts, her petite waist, and the curve of her hips.

Blinded by passion, I pounced, pressing her rear into the wall. She wrapped her arms around my neck, pulling me closer while my lips found the hollow of her throat. I nibbled at her skin, desperate to consume every aspect of her being. My ravenous mouth skimmed southward to the swell of her breast. I lapped the rosy nipple, and she laced her hands into my hair, anchoring me to that position. Seconds ticked by as I sucked at the hardened peak. A moan emitted from her.

My hands snaked to her core, spreading her open and playing with the sensitive spot. Two fingers traced her slick folds, then plunged into her wet depths. She gasped from the onslaught, but her pliant body adjusted. Driven by the need for another release, she rode my fingers. I breathed against her ample breasts, drowning in the scent of arousal and sweat.

The tight control I'd held unraveled. I'd be damned if she came against my hand instead of my cock. Certain she was ready, I withdrew, leaving her whimpering. She leaned against the whitewashed wall, faint streaks of moonlight illuminating her sensual form. My gaze locked cwith hers as I sucked her sweet juices off my digits.

"You really are delicious. I could spend a lifetime devouring you and never get enough." I smirked, then slid off my boots.

Impatient, her hands skated over her breasts and toward her damp curls as she watched me strip from my clothing. She drank me in with a mix of lust and longing that caused my heavy member to twitch. My feet kicked the heap of garments out of my way. I should take her upstairs and properly claim her in my bed, but I couldn't wait.

Unwilling to let her find her climax without me, I approached, grabbed her ass, and lifted her. Instinctively, she snaked her arms over my neck and wrapped her legs around my waist, perfectly lining up my throbbing length with her core. Unable to resist, I pushed forward and filled her to the hilt in one strong thrust. Blood pounded in my ears. Seconds passed as her body adjusted to me.

Sweat beaded my forehead, and the brief respite I afforded her faded with my resolve. Spurred on by desire, I drove into her. The slick slapping of flesh melded with our heavy breaths. Her fingernails dug into my skin, anchoring me to reality. In minutes, the burning sensation built, ready to explode. Yet I held on, certain I'd bring her to another completion.

"I'm so close." Her pupils dilated as she stared at me.

I bucked hard, tilting my hips to hit that responsive spot within her. A moan rippled through her. Her features contorted. She tightened akin to a taut bowstring, seconds from teetering over.

Her muscles contracted, and her body trembled as she plummeted into ecstasy.

"Mateo." She shuddered against me, lost in the moment.

Her cries of rapture tipped me over the edge, and my release spilled into her. I clutched her against me, panting as our hearts beat in unison, melded together in just this instant. We gasped, tangled within one another. Filled with adoration, I placed a kiss on her damp forehead. Her gaze locked with mine, and a hint of her jesting attitude emerged, breaking the intimate moment.

"I'm guessing that is a yes. You want to court me?" She cocked an eyebrow as if our heated entanglement hadn't been evidence enough.

I let out a chuckle. "Yes. I thought you'd never ask."

EPILOGUE

BRIELLE

A SOFT HUM ECHOED through the shop, filling the usually silent space. I cracked the door to the back room open farther, and Naomi's melancholy melody wafted into the tiny rear antechamber. The somber song melded with the punctuating pops from the crackling hearth behind me. Somehow, my life brimmed with constant companionship. With the chit about, she was often chattering about remedies or inquiring over medical techniques throughout the daytime. While I spent my nights with Mateo, as he met all my needs.

The cuckoo-clock ticked above the table, denoting that my time for finishing this remedy was slipping away. My aching fingers scrunched and shifted the pestle from one hand to the other. Forcefully, I pulverized the final ingredient for the elixir for Silas's ever-escalating symptoms. As the herbs turned into a soft powder, I hoped this new concoction would provide him with some ease from his ailment.

Minutes later, with the blend finished, I picked up the mortar and walked to the cauldron boiling over the roaring fire. Slowly, I poured the substance into the brew. Smoke curled in the air, filling the space with an acrid tang. My nostrils burned, but the steam from the elixir caused a lightness to fill my lungs. As I withdrew, allowing the solution to percolate, streaks of red coated my fingertips, as if a trail of blood covered them. I furrowed my brow and wiped my palms clean, staining the once pristine apron with wine-hued stains.

Ding, ding, ding.

The bell chimed, announcing a patron. With Naomi manning the storefront, I remained focused on my task. My gaze flicked to the clock reading noon, and I assumed that Mrs. Johnson was here to pick up her arthritic salve. Seconds passed by while the brew bubbled. Not wanting to overboil the concoction, I grabbed a vial and a ladle that were strewn about the table and strode to the pot. Carefully, I scooped the potion into the vessel. The liquid sloshed. Steam crawled up the thin glass tube as I poured the blood-red remedy until it reached the vial's brim.

The fire crackled, causing sweat to trickle along my temples. Despite the discomfort, I fought the urge to scrub away the sticky perspiration. With the brew secure, I spun and nearly dropped the hour's worth of work as I stared at Mateo. My heart skipped a beat, yet I remained cyeady, slowly walking the tonic to the table. His eyes followed me as I lowered it onto the wooden holder where the concoction would cool.

Once the medicine had been safely stowed, I turned to him. He leaned against the closed door with his hands shoved into his pockets. "Didn't we talk about taking regular breaks?"

His wool coat clung to his shoulders and was buttoned despite the blazing heat within the back room. His hair had lengthened since our first dance at the Kesere festival some months ago at the beginning of winter. Sunlight glimmered through the window, casting light on half his face.

My palms smoothed over my rumpled apron. "You only have yourself to blame. I'm still working on remedies after our afternoon away."

The man hadn't been lying about keeping me in his bed for days. Our interlude had been cut short when young Gregory Smith slipped, fell, and broke his arm on the ice. To my dismay, Naomi had little experience setting bones, forcing her to yank me out of my blissful period after four nights of sheer carnal delight. We'd been inseparable since emerging as a formally courting couple weeks ago.

"Well, you've educated Naomi on the finer practices of wound care and sutures. If another emergency occurs, she is capable of handling it on her own, and you can continue to be trapped in my bed, or on my sofa, or on the kitchen counter." He waggled his eyebrows and grinned from ear to ear.

He sauntered toward me. My pulse skittered. If this tonic hadn't taken hours to concoct, I'd have considered sweeping all the items off my wooden table and letting him take me on it, as he had the day before.

His thumb pressed into my chin, tipping my gaze to him. His voice lowered an octave. "I could devour you, but fear you'd perish from starvation. You barely touched your porridge, and you're trying to work through lunch. What will I do with you?" A smirk crossed his lips.

"You can always punish me. Perhaps a spanking? Or you can tie me up." Desire pulsed through me.

He barked a laugh. "I'm well aware of your delightful proclivities. Maybe later. But I have a surprise I want to show you." He gestured at my stained smock.

Hurriedly, I untied my messy apron and tugged it off, then placed it on the tiny stool near the table. As we exited, the sunlight crested through the shop. I blinked, captivated by the world's beauty in the warm light. My heart pattered in time with his breaths. With each passing day, I suspected I did indeed love this man.

"Thank the gods you're not cavorting in the back room again. You know I can hear you." Naomi closed the journal she often had her nose buried within. She straightened from her lounging position, leaning against the counter. Her lips twisted into a frown, and she glowered at us.

Despite her bluster, a hint of warmth pierced through her icy blue eyes, like the whispers of life were slowly returning to her. Though she and Arianna continued to be on shaky ground, I hoped they'd console each other with the previous loss of their mother and Silas's impending doom.

But the girl would balk at the sympathy I bore for her. Instead, I plastered on my sultry persona and purred, "Poor Naomi. I'm sure there's a chap who'd entertain you, now that you're past your majority. Maybe Vincent." My finger tapped my chin. "He is single and right there in Belmont Manor for the taking."

Naomi snorted. "First, he's far too stiff for me. I desire a bedfellow with a bit more of an edge. Second, I'm not the sister he's pining after."

I cocked my head at her curiously. Then flicked a glance at Mateo, who stared at a hanging snake plant slithering through the rafters. Given his nonchalant expression, he was hiding something from me about the steward.

"Is it possible I'm aware of some gossip before you?" A mischievous grin cut the corner of her mouth.

"Chatting it up with the maids? Perhaps this tiny town of Presspin is growing on you." I grabbed my coat from the hook on the wall behind the counter and slipped it on.

She tugged on the cuff of her crisp white blouse. "It's not. I'm just amusing myself while I'm stuck here. Trust me, I won't be bound to this backwoods village for long."

I pulled out leather gloves and tugged them on. Mateo caught my fingers, lacing ours together again, as if he couldn't bear not touching me for even a moment. Mischief crossed his countenance as he spun to Naomi.

"What a shame. We'll miss your charm. Until then, I'll be occupying Brielle for the afternoon. Be sure to lock up." Mateo breezed past her, tugging me along.

"And take Silas's medicine when you go home," I called out over my shoulder before we exited the shop.

Sunlight glimmered over the snow-covered path, similar to diamonds lining our way. Townspeople bustled about, enjoying this break between storms. The scent of fresh bread wafted from the bakery to our rear, causing my mouth to water. But to my surprise, Mateo didn't tug me toward the square, but in the opposite direction. We weaved through the townspeople who stared at us in shock, certain that the rumors of a settled siren couldn't be true.

Minutes passed, and the clear path ended, leading in the direction of a snow-laden trail with calf-deep slush. My lips pursed at the slippery path weaving through the hundred-foot-tall pines.

"Are you planning to take me against a tree?" I pointed to the grove, uncertain if I'd enjoy being pinned against an icy trunk.

He grinned. "Not until the summer. Perhaps after we've spent the day picnicking and swimming in the pond." He stepped into the snow and pulled me forward.

Curious, I relented and followed his footsteps, keeping myself from sinking into the slushy depths. Birds chirped overhead, singing a mournful tune. Shadows cast over the forest floor from the canopy of branches tangling above. Something unsettling churned in my gut, but I disregarded the sensation as Mateo clung to me, my anchor to this sweeter reality. A quarter of an hour later, we halted beside an evergreen three times the size of those around it. My eyes widened at the massive tree standing akin to a sentinel protecting two gray stones. I stepped closer to read the engravings.

Here lies Ingrid Green, daughter, beloved, and friend.

My breath caught. We were at Ingrid's memory marker. My gaze darted to the stone next to it. But no etching lay on the granite. Instead, it remained unmarred.

"What is this?" I released his hand and approached the unmarked grave. My gloved fingers traced the round curve.

"It's a resting place for your love."

I sucked in a sharp breath.

"I didn't know Wren's surname, and the carver said he'd come in the spring to engrave it for you. I wanted to honor your beloved and provide you a spot to visit her whenever you miss her. She and Ingrid can watch over us from the Great Beyond."

A knot pushed against my windpipe. I'd mentioned to him between throes of passion how challenging courting him would be while Wren hadn't been properly laid to rest. He cared about my worries.

My heart blazed with adoration for Mateo, but it would always ache for Wren. Overwhelmed by the conflicting emotions, my knees buckled, then landed on the icy ground before the marker. A tear rolled down my face, streaking my cheek.

Mateo stepped forward and clamped a hand on my shoulder. With his gentle touch, I came undone, and my sobs burst from me. My shoulders shuddered for long minutes, but I felt no embarrassment as he bore witness to my grief.

My silent sobs melded with the birds' sad songs, like a remembrance ceremony for my lost mate. "I love you, Wren. I'm so sorry I couldn't save you."

"She knows you did everything you could to change what happened. It's all right. She knows," he whispered.

I nodded, partially believing and still slightly unsure of whether she'd forgive me for moving on. But I'd lived this half-life for so long. My gaze flicked to Ingrid's marker, and my palm laid upon it. "Thank you, Ingrid, for drawing me, for choosing me."

My words caught in my throat, because over the weeks, I'd wondered if Ingrid had sketched me to point Mateo in my direction, like a last wish.

Exhausted, Mateo pulled me to my feet and wrapped me in his embrace.

"Was this too much?" He pressed a kiss into my scalp.

"No. It's perfect. I should have done this years ago to honor her. Thank you."

A sea of emotions rolled through his eyes. Perhaps I'd begun falling for him when he'd carried me off from Kesere, or when he cared for my needs or simply listened. As I stared at my mate's mark, a sense of urgency pulled in my soul. Time was too short, and I was unwilling to hide these feelings any longer.

My fingers grazed the soft stubble on his chin. "I love you, Mateo." I nuzzled into the crook of his neck, breathing in his sage and mint scent. "Can we return in the spring and lay flowers on their graves together?"

"Of course, but for now, let's allow them their rest." He released me, but snaked his hand into mine, reuniting our grasps.

As we stood beside the stones, the once bright clouds shifted, casting the scene in an eerie darkness. Mateo tipped his head back, taking in the darkening sky, and frowned. The wind whipped over me, and a shudder dragged down my spine. Gooseflesh rose on my skin, and I froze. My gaze settled upon the blank stone, causing a flicker of panic to beat through me. Perhaps finally laying her to rest was far more than I could bear. But, as always, Mateo yanked me forward, tugging me from the past and into the present, where a mix of light and shadows loomed.

ABOUT THE AUTHOR

CHELLE CYPRESS IS A voracious reader, mother, wife and anime enthusiast. As a child, Chelle dreamed of becoming a published author. Through hard work, many late nights, and copious amounts of coffee, she has finally achieved her dream of sharing the stories of her heart with the world. Chelle infuses her writing with themes from classic literature, regency romances, and fantasy. She enjoys blending the contents together in a novel that she hopes speaks to the hearts of her readers. Chelle has used writing as a therapeutic outlet which has helped her maintain her sobriety (7/30/21).

To follow her on her socials or for upcoming releases:

ACKNOWLEDGEMENT

First, I have to thank my amazing chaos gremlin Tia, because without her this novella wouldn't exist, literally. Mateo and Brielle's relationship plays a decent role in the early events of book two, and after introducing the couple in my rough draft, Tia was curious how their relationship came to pass. From that inquiry, this novella was born. The once simple short story of roughly twelve thousand words quickly morphed into a novella teetering toward a short novel. Thank you, Tia, for your constant help, encouragement, and embracing me not only for my sunshine moments, but also when I am the storm.

Shout out to my alpha and beta readers, April & KT. I appreciate your feedback on such a quick turnaround. Your notes and ideas helped me so much in honing this story.

A huge thank you to my AMAZING developmental editor Brittany Mack with Conquest Publishing. Thank you for taking a deep dive into my world and exploring the depths of these characters' motivations and world. Your notes always help me hone my writing.

Thank you to Amber Thoma for the beautiful cover and encouragement as I navigate the author world.

To my street team Harbingers of Lore, words can't express my gratitude. You've seen my highs and lows and still stuck by me to the end, all while helping me promote my work. Your encouragement, devotion, and help has meant everything to me. Whenever I consider quitting, I think of each and every one of you waiting for my next release. I wouldn't be here without you.

To my readers, thank you for taking yet another chance on me. I know the days are short and there are so many amazing books out there to devour. Thank you for spending time reading mine. I can't wait to share more of this world and the characters in the future.

To my author friends V.H. Faolon, Faith Sloan, and Sabrina Hartley. Thank you for all the writer and life chats. Your encouragement and friendship over the years has meant the world to me. You were with me from the beginning, when Unmasking the Curse was just an idea and have stuck with me ever since.

To Alyssa and Haley for listening to my hyper fixate for yet another year on a new story, for being my two biggest supporters and my best friends. Thank you for the endless hours of Marco Polos coming to my events and propping me up when imposter syndrome tries to tear me down. I can't wait to Marco Polo for you my next novella and novel ideas.

To my husband, Bill. Thank you for always holding space for me, feeding me, encouraging me and reminding me to rest. A certain cinnamon roll in this book may have some of your personality traits. Thank you for seeing me, when I don't see myself.

To my mom and sister, Nicole. Thank you for coming to my events, cheering me on and reminding me I am enough, just as I am.

Finally, to Christy–If I could go back and time to tell you one thing, it would be that you were truly amazing. Your smile was like sunshine, and you could warm even the coldest of souls. Even four years after your passing, I still cry whenever I think about you or hear our song. I still remember the flowers you bought me just because, our long lunches, and walks along the river trail. I wish you were still here, so we can have just one more chat, one more lunch or one more walk. You left a gaping hole in this world that can never be filled. I miss you.